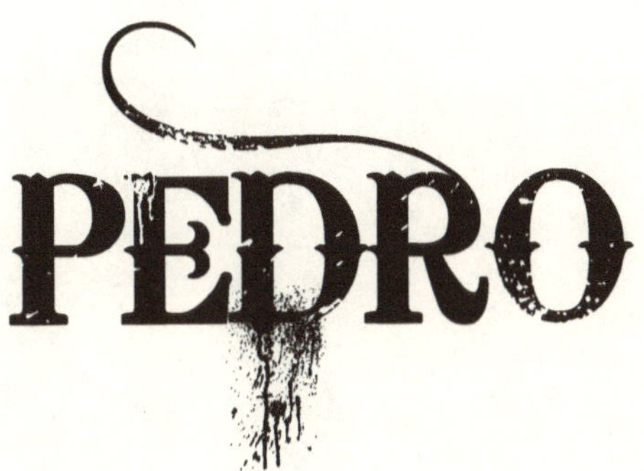

PEDRO

PEDRO

Porn Star Brothers Book 2

L.J. DIVA

★ Royal Star Publishing ★

Chances is an imprint of Royal Star Publishing
www.royalstarpublishing.com.au

This Collector's Edition paperback published in 2018
All Rights Reserved, Copyright ©L.J. Diva 2018

Trade Paperback ISBN: 978-1-925683-43-1
Case Laminate Hardcover ISBN: 978-1-922307-28-6
E-Book ISBN: 978-1-925683-42-4
A catalogue record for this book is available from the National
Library of Australia.

Cover design: Royal Star Publishing and Odyssey Books
Cover photos: CURAphotography/Shutterstock.com
Typesetting in Minion Pro by Royal Star Publishing

 Dedications

In 2014 a vague idea to write a book about a porn star came to me. In 2015 the idea brewed and grew and when my idol, Jackie Collins, passed away, the idea flourished with a vengeance. Jackie Collins is the only inspiration in my life when it comes to writing. She had the passion, the brains, the ballsy rollicking attitude, and the kind of life that made me want to *be* her. Without her, these books would not exist, for I would not have had the inspiration to follow in the same 'write whatever you want' league. Without her, I will continue trying to write the kind of books she wrote. Real, ballsy, and bonkbustingly good.

Jackie, the Porn Star Brothers book series is dedicated to you as so many of my other books are. I thank you for the inspiration you have given me and hope you continue giving me, to go on and write more. I hope that you are well and having a good laugh wherever you are. I miss you and will continue doing so. Sometimes I think I feel you egging me on with my writing. Maybe that's true, and maybe it's just my rampant imagination; the same imagination that has given me the books I have written so far in my life. And sometimes, I really wished I could be you. You will forever be my idol and inspiration and I thank you. RIP, Miss Jackie C.

And to the three Stefanovic brothers, Carlos, Pedro, and Tomas, without whom I would not have had names for my porn stars.

PEDRO

June 1977

Thumping music reverberated through Santorini's biggest and most popular dance club and into the night. The crowd was high on life and bouncing up and down with an energy seen only in addicts. The floor shook with the momentum of their fervent dancing and was slick with five hours of sweat and lust.

Club owner, Andros Poulos, looked on from his private enclosed balcony above the dance floor. Night after night the place was packed to the rafters with frenzied club hoppers and party goers. Night after night they bought his drinks, his women, his blow. And it was all because of one man.

Pedro Stephanopoulos.

The hot twenty-year-old stud had become a DJ sensation the year before on Mykonos and Andros had been able to get him this summer. Because word had gotten around, all the tourists from all the islands came to Santorini every night. And it was only the first month of summer.

He gazed across the electric scene before him; Pedro dancing on stage throwing the beats together, women gyrating and thrusting down the front trying to get his attention. So were some of the men. The rest of the crowd was an eclectic mix of men, women, locals, tourists, gays and straights, all blending like an exotic cocktail of spice, lust and sex.

Andros watched Pedro. The hot stud had everything going for him. Six feet of rock-hard body and jet-black hair with locks hanging over his bright blue eyes. His toned chest glistened with sweat under the lights, and his white shirt hung open, plastered to his body. White pants were slung low, allowing everyone to dream of what he held there. Waving his arms in the air, he encouraged the crowd to yell and scream.

Yes, Pedro Stephanopoulos was a very good investment indeed.

"Papa." Angelina, Andros's daughter, came up beside him.

He was so proud of his baby girl. At eighteen she had finished high school with top honours and had a scholarship to Juilliard in New York. It was not that he couldn't afford to send her, as he was one of the wealthiest men on the island, but she had earned her seat all on her own. Now she was spending the summer with him before leaving in the fall. "Angelina, how do you like the place?" It was her first visit to the club and he wanted to make an impression.

"Noisy," she said, tucking a strand of hair behind her ear. "The bright lights are giving me a headache." The petite girl with her long black hair, big brown eyes, and perfect complexion stood beside her father shielding her eyes.

"Come, come." He ushered her into his office and closed the door. The noise dropped away and the air was almost silent.

"Ah, that's better." She sat on the sofa. "Too noisy for me."

"And yet you're moving to New York, a city that never sleeps," her father argued. "*And* attending a music school. And yet this…" He waved an arm toward the club. "This is too noisy for you?"

She smiled. "Papa, it won't be so noisy at the school, and I'll be staying in a quiet part of the city, so I'll get plenty of peace and quiet."

"Do you have to go?" Andros sat beside her and placed a hand over hers. "Do I have to lose my little girl?"

"Papa." She patted his hand. "You're not losing me. I'm going to further my education."

"Of course I'm losing you." He kissed her hand. "It's not as if you're going to the mainland to school. You're going half way around the world for God's sake. I won't be able to see you unless I fly there."

"And what's wrong with that?"

He sighed. "Nothing. Not if it means my little girl is getting the best education she can." Andros paused and then leant toward her. "Are you *sure* you want to go?"

Angelina laughed. "Of course, Papa. I'm going, and *that's final.*"

He got up and wandered over to the balcony door.

"Well, if there's nothing more I can say," he said lightly, half joking. "Then you should go. There's nothing here for you, only too much noise, too much light."

She smiled at his attempted joke. "Okay, Papa. I still have another month before I go. I'll see you tomorrow." She kissed him on the cheek and left. Stopping at the bottom of the stairs she gazed toward the stage where Pedro was, admiring the tall, bare-chested stud. He barely glanced in her direction, but she still felt the thrill of that glance go down to her soul. He wouldn't be the first man she'd bedded, but he was definitely going to be the one before she left for college.

Pedro waved his arm in the air, drawing cheers from the crowd. It was a hot night. A steamy 100 degrees created a lot of sweat and a lot of drinking. He slowed things down with another track and took a few moments to down a bottle of water. "Ladies and gentlemen, I wanna see you get your groove thang on, slow it down now." He danced behind his console, gave his headphones a wipe and downed another bottle of water that Mikos, the bartender, had brought him.

Mikos hovered by the side of the stage. "You need anything else, Peds?" he yelled.

"How 'bout a bottle of juice and something to eat?" Pedro yelled back. "I need to keep my energy up and I'm sweating out the water."

Mikos nodded and hurried away. Part of his job that summer was to make sure Pedro had everything he needed to do the job he had to do. It was his first job and he wanted to make an impression on the boss. At eighteen, and fresh out of school, he needed the job and the money, *and* he got paid extra for taking care of Pedro. So why would he mind? He minded because Pedro got all the girls. Not that he was overly interested in them, but Mikos knew that by hanging around Pedro that maybe he'd get a few girls coming his way.

He grabbed a large jug of juice and poured it into a glass bottle, added a basket of mini burgers and fries to the tray and took them back to the stage, leaving them on the small table behind the DJ booth.

Pedro noticed and waved before turning his attention to the girls down the front. His fingers did a little wave and he winked, sending them into a screaming frenzy, waving their hands back at him. One even bared her breasts.

God, life was good as a DJ!

That girl was still there three hours later when he finished, and she cornered him outside as he was taking a breather.

"Oh, Pedro, you're so hot." She sidled up to him and ran her fingers across his chest. "I want you."

A part of him was surprised, even though the rest of him wasn't. It was something he'd been getting for the last month. Women wanting him, men wanting him, it was turning into a summer frenzy of sex, love and holiday romance.

"That's nice," he said, finishing off his juice and trying to be polite. "Glad you enjoyed yourself. I'm off home." He left the bottle at the back door and took off for the beach. After the night he'd had he needed a swim to cool off, and peeling off the sweat soaked shirt that was plastered to his body, he dropped it on the sand. His pants were stiff and dry against his skin from hours of sweaty dancing, so he dropped those as well and stood in his bare flesh.

Summer time on the islands, middle of the night, no one was going to care that he was naked.

He ran for the water and dived in, relishing the coolness on his hot flesh. He did a few strokes to the left, a few strokes to the right, and floated on his back looking up at the sky. It was as if he was part of it, floating in blackness surrounded by stars. He felt himself drift off but pulled himself back. Not a good place to fall asleep. Swimming for the shore he saw a white figure on the sand where his clothes were, and stepping out of the water he noted the figure was a woman.

"Pedro," she sing-songed.

He walked over to her and saw the woman from the club, stark naked and voluptuously curvy. He stirred. "You followed me?"

She noticed the stirring. "Yes. I want you." She threw herself at his chest, and he caught her by the arms. "Take me, I want you, I'm yours." She flattened her body against him and her hot flesh melded with his.

He stirred more, hardening between her open thighs.

Her lips hovered below his, and her hand reached down to guide him, pulling him down to the sand and inside of her, groaning as he entered, cocooned in her warmth. She arched into him, and his mouth inhaled her breast, sucking, licking, biting, teasing it into submission. She came, and he kept thrusting.

"You need to put your clothes back on."

Her eyes opened, and she saw him doing his pants up. "What?" She was confused. *Wasn't he just inside of me making love to me?* "What are you doing?"

"Getting dressed. I just took a swim and now I'm going home. You need to put your clothes on." He nodded at her dress on the sand. "I'm flattered, but not interested." He picked up his shirt, shoes and bag and headed for the dock. He was taking the ferry home to Mykonos for some good food and good sleep.

"What do you mean you're not interested?" she screamed and ran after him. "I'm offering you my body." She jumped in front of him and grabbed her breasts. "I'm offering you these, *this*, on a platter and *you're turning me down*? What?" She cocked her top lip. "Don't like pussy? What are you, a fag?"

Pedro gave her a dirty look. "No, I'm not. I'm just not interested in *you*." He continued on his way, but she attacked him.

"How dare you," she screamed and pushed him down from behind. He fell to the sand and she pounced, planting herself on him, rolling him over and ripping at his zip. "How dare you refuse me?" He grabbed at her hands, but she'd already pulled his cock out and was trying to sit on it. "How dare you."

He got her by the arms and threw her off, sending her rolling across the sand. Getting to his feet, he grabbed his things and ran, pulling up his zip along the way. Making it to the ferry as it pulled in, he reported the woman to the ferry master, who called over a wharf officer.

"What happened?" the officer asked.

"She attacked me because I wouldn't have sex with her." Pedro put his shoes on and examined the red marks on his torso and arms. "I'm a DJ at SantorPoulos, the club owned by Andros Poulos. She was there all night and followed me down to the beach. Then she attacked me when I told her I wasn't interested. She followed me. She's crazy, crazy man." He saw they weren't taking him all that seriously, although, at the mention of his boss, they had perked up. "I seriously doubt *my boss* is going to like the fact his patrons are attacking his staff."

"Of course, of course," the officer said. While he didn't know Andros Poulos personally, his chief did. "Tell me, a description of her."

"Average height, a mop of brown hair, curvy figure." Pedro shrugged. "That's about it. Don't know her name. She wasn't Greek, so probably a tourist."

The officer took notes. "Of course. So many tourists on this island. It will be hard to find her. We will keep a lookout for a woman matching that description and see if she attacks other men." He nodded. "Mr Stephanopoulos."

Pedro sighed. He knew he wasn't going to get any help from the police whatsoever, so he jumped on board the ferry and headed home, watching the sun rise over the horizon, sending the sky into a rainbow of colours. After a nice hot shower and an equally hot breakfast, he was going to sleep all day.

He got off the boat and walked home, arriving to find his house in an uproar. "Mama, Papa, what's wrong?" He saw Tomas sitting on the sofa next to his grandparents, stunned into silence.

"Wrong?" Spiros yelled. "Wrong! What's wrong is your brother has gone and shot someone and raped two women."

Pedro turned Tomas. "Tomas, how could—"

"Not him," Spiros roared. "Carlos." He paced back and forth across their small lounge room.

Pedro stared at his parents. "What? Wait, are you saying that Carlos…no…he wouldn't."

"And now he has disappeared and no one knows where he's gone," Jenny said, tears sliding silently down her face. "The police were here last night. They ripped the place apart looking for him. I've only just finished tidying everything." Her eyes went around the room.

Pedro shook his head. "No…I can't…no…he wouldn't." He looked at his brother. "Tomas?"

Tomas finally looked up, a desolate expression on his face. "What?"

"Do *you* know what happened? You work at the same resort."

Tomas inhaled slowly then exhaled, his head moving from side to side. "I have no idea. I was on the other side of the resort. I heard there had been gunshots and that the masseur was involved. Nothing else." His mind wandered off again.

Pedro ran a hand through his hair and felt the sand and grit in it.

His mother saw him. "You go," she said. "Go and have a shower and I'll make you some breakfast." She waved him toward the boys' private quarters. "Go freshen up and I'll make your favourite. Go." Looking around at nothing, she finally moved from her spot in the middle of the room.

Pedro saw the scene around him and took off, seeking refuge under the spray of cold then hot water. He alternated between the two as he soaped himself down and washed off the dry sweat and salty grit. He thought about Carlos.

What in the hell had he gotten himself into? Were the cops *really* after him for rape and a shooting? It was well known that Carlos loved women and was paid to please them; he didn't need to force a woman into sex. And shooting? Carlos had never held a gun in his life. None of them had. Not even back in Australia when they were kids. Their parents had wanted nothing to do with guns, so they'd never learned how to shoot.

He turned off the taps and stepped out. Wrapping the towel around his waist, he wondered what this meant now. *Are the cops hunting him down? Where is he? What really happened? Is he still on the island? What if they catch him? Who were the women? Why was there a shooting? And most importantly, who got shot?*

He quickly dressed in the shorts and tank he slept in and started feeling the effects of needing sleep, barely making it into the dining room just as breakfast was ready.

"Eat up." Jenny placed a plate of eggs, bacon and sausages in front of him and lovingly slid her hand over his hair. "You're still a growing boy, you need your strength." She planted a kiss on his forehead.

Tomas sat down morosely and picked at his toast.

"What's wrong with you?" Pedro wasn't sure he could down so much food just yet, so poured himself a tall glass of juice.

Tomas gazed at him. "Huh?"

"Jesus, you're out of it." Pedro finished his drink and dug into his food.

Tomas shrugged a shoulder and went back to picking at his toast.

Spiros finally made it to the table. "Our son may have ruined his life, but he will *not* ruin ours. We will try to stick to our normal routine. Breakfast, lunch and dinner. Meat shop, home. He will *not* ruin our lives too."

"Do we actually *know* what happened?" Pedro asked as his mother and grandparents sat down with their own food.

"He raped and shot, enough said," Spiros spat.

"Except, Carlos *wouldn't do that, none of us* would. You raised us better than that," Pedro argued. "He *wouldn't* do that."

"*Well, he did.*" Spiros slammed a hand down on the table. "He did, end of story. Eat your breakfast."

"Well, *I* don't believe it," Pedro replied, defying his father. "We know Carlos, you raised him, he wouldn't rape a woman any more than me or Tomas would. And why would he shoot anyone? Who did he supposedly shoot and why should we believe anything the cops say? They're just as corrupt here as on the mainland."

"Because he ran away like a gutless coward after he did it. That is not a son I raised." Spiros's face was as black as thunder. "That is no son of mine."

"How do we know he ran away?" Pedro demanded. "He could be hiding out until he can tell his side of the story."

"Because he left us a letter," Jenny said quietly.

Pedro zeroed in on her. "What?"

She looked up. "He left a letter on the table. I found it before the police got here."

"What does it say?" Pedro asked eagerly. "Read it."

She slipped it out of her dress pocket and handed it to him. He read it out loud. "If you're reading this then I've gone. I've been planning to leave for some time, using my twenty-fifth birthday as the date I travel overseas to a new land. But if I'm not twenty-five then something has happened to make me leave. I've left some money toward expenses and hope all is safe and well with all of you as it may not be with me. Don't worry, it'll be fine, love Carlos."

"Sounds like he already had that prepared," Tomas finally piped up.

"Sounds like he has no idea what's going on," Pedro replied. "No mention of the current problem. Look…" He gazed at his parents. "Something is clearly wrong and we need to find out what actually happened."

"No." Spiros banged the table as he stood. "No more talk of him. No more." He shoved back his chair and stormed out of the house.

"But, Mama—" Pedro started.

"Stop," she said sadly, patting her son on the hand. "Just finish your breakfast and get some rest. You have work again tonight, don't you?"

"Yes, Mama."

"Then finish up and rest." She went back to eating her own food.

Pedro exhaled loudly and returned to his food, finishing what he could before hitting the bed in his room. He was physically tired, but his brain was racing. He needed sleep and needed to calm down. *Breathe in slowly, and out slowly.* He thought about being attacked and how it must have gone down with Carlos. *Breathe in slowly, and out slowly.* He thought about his parents and wondered what the hell was with Tomas. *Breathe in slowly…breathe out slowly…*

His alarm went off at six p.m., and his eyes flew open. "Oh." He took a deep breath, jumped out of bed and changed. Walking into the lounge room, he found his mother wringing her hands.

"Don't worry, Mama, it will all work out. Carlos will come home. This will be sorted. We'll all be together again."

She smiled, but it didn't reach her eyes.

He kissed her cheek and left for the ferry, sailing across the water and making it to Santorini by seven-thirty.

"Mikos," Pedro greeted. "I'm going to need a bodyguard

tonight, as well as lots of food and drink."

"What's this about a bodyguard?" Andros questioned as he patted Pedro on the shoulder. "Does my resident DJ need protection?" He took the seat beside Pedro at the bar.

"I'll say," Pedro said. "Some crazy woman from last night followed me down to the beach and was standing naked for me when I got out after my swim. Then she started screaming when I told her I wasn't interested and ran after me, pushed me down and scratched me." He showed the red marks on his skin. "Then she pulled my cock out of my pants and tried to sit on it. I pushed her away and ran for the wharf to tell the officer what had happened. Unless I see her again and point her out they probably won't catch her."

Mikos shook his head. "Dude, that was some wild cat. She was buck naked waiting for you?" He could only guess what Pedro Stephanopoulos looked like in the downstairs department, but if his brother Carlos was any indication of the family genes, then Pedro was packing heat as well. Not that he'd intentionally set out to see Carlos naked, he'd just happened to be sneaking around the masseur's cabana and heard a woman screaming out 'more, more' and had been curious enough to take a peek. There was Carlos in all his Greek Australian glory of ten inches of thick, strong muscle. Mikos had watched him enter the woman over and over, pleasing, pleasuring, making her groan and writhe on the massage table. It had turned him on so much he had to relieve himself in the bushes before leaving. It was not as though he had a girlfriend to take it out on, so the bushes and his hand had to do. He wondered if Pedro did the same things.

"Well, my boy, we'll just have to hire a guard to walk you to the ferry and back. Can't have any more women attacking my star attraction," Andros said. "The club opens in a few minutes; why don't you go and get ready?"

Pedro took his water bottle and clambered up on stage. He already had his set list ready, as he planned them a week ahead, so he gathered the records together ready to play. He hadn't mentioned anything about Carlos, and didn't even know if the news had travelled, but Greek islands were like Greek villages; news got around pretty damn fast.

He set up the first record, an extended 12 inch that was going to play for a good twenty minutes. He always started with something simple as the doors opened at eight, but the place wasn't really going until eight-thirty when his gig started, so they played music while people settled in and got warmed up.

The doors opened and he set the needle on it.

This time also gave him a few minutes to eat and psyche himself up. And tonight he needed psyching. He loved music and desperately wanted to be a world-renowned DJ, but whatever the hell was going on with Carlos had got him out of sync.

Finishing his food, he swallowed the last of his juice and stood to get himself limber. After shaking his shoulders and stretching his arms above his head to stretch his back out, he swung his arms around in circles and jumped on the spot, loosening up every muscle he had for the onslaught of his performance. He needed to get all thought of everything, and everyone, out of his brain, preferring to start each show with a clear mind and body.

Last night popped into his head. What in God's name had possessed that woman to follow him, get naked and expect sex, then attack him and try and sit on his cock? What the hell was in her head that she wanted to sit on him and was going to assault him for it? He shook his head. He didn't know, but he didn't like it, and he hoped she didn't turn up tonight. He peered through the curtain and saw her front and centre.

"Shit!" He thought for a moment. "Hey, Mikos," he yelled and waved the bartender over. "Tell Poulos that crazy woman from last night is here again and ask if I can get one of the bouncers to keep an eye on her."

"Sure thing." Mikos walked off, and ten minutes later, just before Pedro was set to go on stage, one of the bouncers came behind the curtain.

"Mr P said to guard you against some crazy woman?"

"She's crazy all right." Pedro pointed her out to the bouncer. "Keep an eye on her for me." He took to the stage and grabbed the mic. "Ladies and gentlemen. Welcome to Club SantorPoulos. I am Pedro Stephanopoulos your DJ, are you ready to rock tonight?" He waved his arm in the air. A chorus of screaming came back at him. "Then let's get down to the funky beats of The Trammps and *Disco Inferno.*"

The night went from there, and he finished up ten hours later with a resounding rendition of Thelma Houston's *Don't Leave Me This Way* that had the whole club singing at the top of their lungs and wildly, drunkenly, waving their arms in the air.

Pedro set up the system to play a 12 inch to take them out for the rest of the morning until the club shut, then left the stage.

"Here." Mikos handed him a burger and bottle of juice. "Rehydrate."

Pedro took the bottle and swallowed half the juice before taking a breath. "God I am so hot," he whooped. "Everybody loves me." He waved his arms in the air and did a little dance. "Everybody loves me, yeah, yeah," he sang. "Everybody loves me, yeah, yeah."

Andros came backstage. "They certainly do. The club is full every night that you're here. Are you sure I can't convince you to work seven nights a week?" He straightened his suit and eyed the stallion before him. Thank God Angelina didn't come to the club.

Pedro shook his head. "Nah, man. I need time off to party and have some fun. Four nights is enough for me."

"Yes. I'm sure it is. Especially now."

Pedro stopped dancing. "What? Why now?"

"Well, with your brother and everything..." Andros gave a slight shrug. "Do you need time off?"

Pedro licked his lips. "What do you mean? What about my brother?"

Andros checked his watch. "Well, it's just that..." He waved a hand. "It's gotten out that Carlos assaulted two women and shot one."

Pedro's temper flared and he grabbed Poulos by the collar. "Don't you dare talk rubbish about my brother like that, he did no such thing. He would never hurt a woman like that. We were raised better than that."

Andros's bodyguard pulled Pedro off his boss and twisted his arm up behind his back.

"Ow, get off me."

"It's all right, Magnus, let him go. Clearly the whole deal about his brother has him upset," Andros said and waved his bodyguard off. "Clearly Mr Stephanopoulos is close to his family and very upset by the current events, but if he ever," he stepped close to Pedro, "touches me that way again, with violence in his mind," his eyes flashed, "then he will need a lesson in etiquette. Has he got that clear?" The threat in his voice made it very clear.

Pedro glared darkly at him and brushed down his shirt. "Yeah, things are *very* clear now." Grabbing his bag, he stormed out the back door and down to the beach for a swim.

Stripping off, he waded into the cool calming water and swam out to the platform that was for tourists to lie on. He climbed up and spread out, flat on his back, looking up at the sky. Yeah, he got Andros's message loud and clear. He didn't mind using you but if you crossed him, look out.

After a few more minutes in which he formulated a plan, Pedro swam back, collected his things, and headed for the ferry.

*****

Pedro had the next three days off, so he went in search of Carlos. He went to the resort and spoke to all of his co-workers.

Antonio had no idea where he was, but had noted that his mother had disappeared without a word at the same time. She had since called to let him know she was back in Los Angeles dealing with some things.

He spoke to some of the maids who were working that night and all reported hearing the same thing. A scream, a gunshot, another scream, and then some big hubbub followed. And no one had seen Carlos since. Many speculated about what had happened, what he'd done, *if* he'd done it, and who the person was who'd been shot, but no one could categorically come up with a definite timeline, or had any proof to show for that night.

Pedro scoured the streets, the paths, the windmills, even took the ferry to all of the islands to see if Carlos was hiding out, it was all to no avail, so he went to the last place he wanted to go.

The police station.

"I'd like to talk to the detective in charge of the shooting at the Mykonos Desert Resort."

The officer eyed him up and down. "And what is your interest?"

Pedro sighed. "You're investigating my brother for the crime."

The officer, a tall, thin man with a thin moustache, stopped leaning on the counter and stood straight.

"*You* are the brother?"

"Yes. Just get the officer in charge, please," Pedro snapped.

"*I* am the officer in charge."

Pedro turned to see a fat man of Greek descent, maybe mid-fifties, with a fat face and sweaty complexion. "Good. I want to talk to you about the charges you have against my brother from the Mykonos Desert Resort."

"And why do you need to know? Besides being his brother."

"Because I want to know what you know." Pedro got impatient. "What charges are you bringing against him, and what are you doing to prove his innocence and solve the case?"

"What we are doing, Mr Stephanopoulos is of no concern to you, regardless of the fact it's your brother we are investigating."

"I have a right to know," Pedro stated.

"No, Mr Stephanopoulos, you do not. Now leave my station or I will have you for obstruction."

"Obstruction?" Pedro laughed. "How am I obstructing anything? Are you kidding?"

"No, Mr Stephanopoulos. I am not. Now leave." The cop's hand went to his belt.

Pedro finally noticed the other officers had gathered and frowned. "Mmm," he mumbled. Something was definitely going on here. "I'll leave," he said. "But I don't like the fact no one will tell us what's happened to Carlos." He left and headed home.

The officer ushered his co-workers away and went

back to his office where he dialled a number and waited for the call to connect. "We have the young one sniffing around…yes…yes…all right. I will." He hung up and told one of his constables to tail Pedro Stephanopoulos.

*****

Pedro was back at work Wednesday night, fuming over a wasted three days. There was no sign of Carlos, no one knew anything or saw anything. The cops weren't co-operating, and a wall of silence had gone up.

And now he had Andros to deal with.

"I want you to work more nights," he told Pedro before work.

"I told you no. My contract's for four nights, and that's it." Pedro sorted through the records and put them in order of play.

Mikos brought in a burger and juice for Pedro's preshow meal and was waved away by Andros.

"You mean *this* contract?" There was a tearing sound.

Pedro looked up to see Poulos holding two pieces of ripped paper.

"You don't have a contract," Andros said. "So, now you work the whole week."

Pedro got angry and stood up. "If I don't have a contract then I don't work *any* night of the week. Guess I shouldn't be here now." He stepped off stage, but Andros stopped him with a hand on his chest.

"I was just joking."

Pedro glanced from his hand to him. "Were you?"

Andros removed his hand. "Of course. I was just testing you." There was a slight nervousness in his voice. "I really want you here every night, Pedro. I'd even give you a raise to be here."

Pedro picked up the burger. "I told you. I need time off to have a life. Four nights is enough." He went back to sorting the records, his back to Andros.

Andros seethed under his tightly starched collar. *No one does this to me, Andros Poulos. Oh, no, not without consequences.* He pulled a small vial out of his pocket and quickly tipped the powder it contained into the bottle of juice. "Well, that's a pity." He pocketed the vial. "We could have made lots of money."

Pedro turned around. "Don't you already?"

Andros smiled his Cheshire cat grin. "Of course, but we could always make more." His fingers played with the vial in his pocket. "I'll let you get on with it." He left the backstage area and walked through the club, shaking hands with the first patrons through the doors, and made his way up to his office to watch the show. And what a show it would be.

Pedro started the night's festivities. "Ladies and gentlemen, welcome to SantorPoulos, here on Santorini. It's hot out there, it's hot in here, so let's see how much hotter we can make it. Let's party."

The crowd screamed. The place was packed as it was every night he was there, and he saw the woman who had attacked him front and centre.

He played for half an hour then sculled back the

juice, not realising the special ingredient. The room spun as fast as the disco balls. The lights flashed before his eyes. He was euphoric. Higher than he'd ever felt before. Like he could fly.

He closed his eyes and danced freely behind his console. The hours passed in moments and he was even more lost in the beat. He laid down a 12-inch track, removed his headphones and jumped into the crowd to dance.

All the women screamed and gathered around him, bumping and grinding with him, *against* him. The brunette woman pulled his shirt off so he was bare, and all the women reached out to lay a hand on him.

They gyrated as one, waving their hands in the air, whooping and hollering to the music. He was high on life, free as a bird, and had never felt this way in his life. He didn't know where it came from, or what it was, but he knew he wanted more.

He took to the stage for more beats and ended the night before jumping off stage to knock back the water Mikos had left for him. "Woohoo," he yelled. *"That was awesome!"*

Mikos came back in. "Here's some food. You burnt a lot of energy up there."

"Woohoo." Pedro danced around. "That was freaking awesome. Oh, God, I felt so free." He grabbed the burger and all but inhaled it.

Mikos shook his head. "I don't know how you do it, man. You eat burgers all night and still look like that."

"It's because of the en.a.gee," Pedro stated. "I burn it all off under those lights. Whoo. I'm gonna go for a swim. You wanna come?" He grabbed his bag and headed out the back door.

"No. I gotta finish up here." Mikos's voice trailed off. "Don't wait for me..." He had another couple of hours to go anyway.

Pedro raced down to the water, stripped off, and dived in. It felt good on his hot skin, and a few laps wore him out. "Man, I gotta get home and get me some sleep."

He headed for the wharf and took the ferry home where he found the place quiet and dark, and after a shower fell asleep in bed.

*****

Angelina Poulos had her eye on the DJ at her father's club. He didn't know who she was yet as they hadn't met, but she planned on changing that very soon. She pulled the skimpy crocheted dress she planned on wearing when she introduced herself to Pedro from her wardrobe. He would take one look at her and not want anyone else. She slipped it over her head and pulled it down over her bottom. Flesh in all the right places. Holes for her nipples to poke through, if the need called for it because she was not wearing anything under it. Stepping into high strappy red heels, she fluffed out her hair and eyed herself in the full-length mirror.

Sex on legs with dangerous curves in all the right places.

*****

The alarm blared in Pedro's ear at 6 p.m.

"Ugh." He half woke, groggy, dizzy, tired. "Ugh." He knew he had to get up for work, but the pounding headache made him want to stay in bed.

The alarm went on and on, and his mother came in. "Pedro?" She saw him half awake and leaning up on his elbow. "You don't look good." Moving to her son's side, she felt his forehead and cheeks. "You're not burning up." She looked into his dull blue eyes. "Maybe you're coming down with something?"

"I don't feel good," he mumbled. "But I gotta get up for work." He sat on the side of the bed and put his head in his hands. "Ugh."

"I'll get you something." Jenny left and came back with aspirin and juice. "Take these, they'll help."

He downed four and freshened up. "Ugh. I gotta go. Love you, Mama." He kissed her on the cheek and headed for the ferry.

Two hours later, he opened the show, and half an hour later, he was downing the bottle of juice that Mikos had left and that Andros had left the special ingredient in.

Half an hour later, he was high as a kite and feeling so good he got down into the crowd again. The women loved him and adored him and gyrated against him. He floated back up on stage and danced to the music in his head before downing another bottle of juice.

That's when he saw her.

Standing backstage, a hot sexy number in a hot sexy red dress. Hair down to her sexy ass, and sexy tits that had sexy nipples poking through the holes in the dress.

He eyed her, laid down a 12-inch track, and danced off stage into the side room to her. "Well, hello." He kept moving as she moved with him.

"Hello, yourself," she purred, thrusting her breasts forward so her nipples were prominent through the material.

He spied them, and the fact she wasn't wearing anything under such a see-through dress made him hard.

She slid the dress up little by little as she danced against him.

The erotic closeness made his heart pound and his cock ache, more so when she unzipped his pants.

He towered over her by half a head and the heat of intimacy at the moment was multiplied by a million.

She pulled him out and massaged him.

He breathed hard.

She pulled her dress up to her hips to show her offering.

He breathed harder.

She rolled a condom on him.

He breathed, turned her, and had her against the table, gripping it as he took her from behind. In time with the pounding beats of the music, he thrust, and she met those thrusts, grinding, grating against him, her breath coming in short gasps.

He had her by the hips, but she moved his left hand up to her breast. Her nipple seized the moment and surged through the hole in the dress and into his waiting hand. She made him squeeze it and grunted some more.

The song came to its crescendo, and so did they.

Pedro gasped and grabbed the bottle of water from the table. He knocked it back while still inside of her, waiting until he drank the last drop before exiting. He stumbled back. "Ugh," he puffed. "Oh, God."

Angelina flicked her hair over her shoulder, slid her dress down, turned around and zipped him up. "Time for you to get back on stage."

He shook his head and took a deep breath, having no grasp on what or how or who had just happened, but he liked it. Getting back on stage, he stumbled behind his console. He was woozy, light headed, but still managed to get the next record on.

Andros noticed from his office. "Magnus, get another bottle of juice down to Mr Stephanopoulos. It looks like he needs some refreshment."

Magnus nodded and left the room.

Andros watched him walk across the club, get the juice from Mikos, and take it backstage. A few moments later he walked back out. Andros watched Pedro's behaviour for the rest of the night.

*****

Pedro didn't see the girl again until Saturday night after he finished work and was heading to the beach for his nightly swim. "Hey, it's you." He saw her waiting at the sand. "From last night."

"Hello, Pedro," Angelina murmured seductively, moving her scarcely bikini clad, very curvy, very sensual body.

He greedily eyed her figure. "I didn't see you after that, uh…"

"Fuck session."

His brows went up. "If that's what you want to call it."

She seductively moved over to him and trailed her finger up his sweat soaked chest. "That's what it was, and that's what I want again."

He hardened. "Where do you want it?"

She looked around. "How about here. I can't wait."

"On the beach?" He glanced around. "We'll be seen."

"How about out on the platform? I'll race you." She ran for the water and dived in. He chased her, dropping his bag and clothes before slicing through the cooling water to the platform out on the ocean. He made it as she climbed out and saw her quickly untie her bikini straps to reveal her luscious naked body. She lay down, arched her breasts, put her arms over her head, and held her legs together.

He knelt above her and spread her legs which she willingly moved.

"Don't forget protection." She handed him a condom, and he rolled it on before sliding into and onto her. Her body felt so right against his as he smoothly and assuredly moved inside of her as he feasted upon her body.

She led him, guided him, showed him what to do. "Oh, God Pedro, oh, God," she cried into the night as he sped up. Her legs wrapped around him, her nails dug into his back.

"Ugh." He grunted and delved his tongue into her willing mouth.

"Ugh," they groaned together until he was done.

He collapsed on top of her, and she held him tight until he leant up on one elbow, his head in his hand. He stroked her hair, her face, her lips. "Who are you, you wicked woman?"

She smiled as seductively as she moved. Everything was seductive about her, and he was captured and enraptured by it. "I'm a woman who knows what she wants."

"And a woman who clearly *gets* what she wants," Pedro said. His watch beeped. "Fuck, I gotta go or I'll miss the ferry." He slid out of her and picked up her bikini. "Last one back." He dived into the water and was halfway back before she even got off the platform.

He was zipping up his pants when she emerged like a goddess from the water and casually walked over to him.

She took her bikini and tied it up.

"I gotta go." He picked up his bag. "Will I see you again?"

"Of course." She ran her tongue over his torso. "You don't think I'd walk away from this do you?"

He grinned, relieved by her words. "Good. I gotta go." He was in the shower an hour later, when Tomas walked into the bathroom.

"Hurry up, little brother, I need the shower."

Pedro turned off the tap and stepped out, grabbing the towel Tomas handed him. "Doesn't anyone get any privacy anymore?" He picked up his electric razor and started shaving.

"Whoa!" Tomas's wide eyes were looking at his brother's back. "What have you been up to, or should I say, *who* have you been up?"

Pedro glanced at him. "What do you mean?" He saw his brother's gaze on his back and turned around to look in the mirror. Red nail marks were on his back. "Fuck!" he muttered. "Didn't know they were there."

"Who is she?" Tomas started brushing his teeth.

Pedro sighed. "Don't know."

Tomas raised a brow. "You had sex with a woman and you don't know who she is or what her name is? What does she look like? How long have you known her? Where does she come from?"

Pedro sighed again. "Yes, petite, curvy, long black hair and gorgeous, two days, and don't know."

"Jesus, Pedro." Tomas paused his brushing. "You met a girl two days ago and don't know her name. Do you know if she's even legal?"

Pedro stopped with wide eyes. "Uh, no. I *think* she is. She definitely knows what she's doing."

"Just because she knows what she's doing doesn't mean she's old enough to be doing it. Jesus, Pedro," Tomas repeated. "You finished? Get out." He shoved his brother out the door.

*****

Andros Poulos sat behind his desk. His plan was working, but it needed time and needed co-operation. With his daughter moving to New York in a couple of weeks, he needed Pedro to work seven days a week to bring in the money. Not that his side businesses of sex and drugs didn't, but he wanted more. *Needed* more. Everyone wanted drugs. Everyone *needed* drugs. And Pedro was going to help him with that even if he never knew it.

*****

The brunette woman who had attacked Pedro sat in her room at Santorini's Bellisima Hotel. It was far from the best accommodation, but she didn't need the best, just the cheapest. She rifled through the photos of Pedro that she'd taken. Him at the club, on the beach, in Mykonos, at home. Yes, she knew where he lived, knew he had two brothers, knew one was now missing, and knew he was the man she wanted for a husband and as the father of her children.

Yes, she would get Pedro Stephanopoulos in her bed if it was the last thing she did. She looked at the letter she'd received from a lawyer, threatening her with a lawsuit if she didn't stop stalking some guy she'd fucked. Screwing up the paper she threw it into the rubbish bin where it landed next to the empty box of brown hair dye.

*****

After three days off with a pounding headache, Pedro couldn't wait to get back to the club to lay down his tracks. It lifted him, in ways he didn't think other people could imagine, especially lately. Getting lost in the sounds, the bass, the melodies, had helped him deal with the situation with Carlos and now he needed a fix.

Having knocked back his regular burger and bottle of juice, he proceeded to get the crowd high on life. He spied Angelina backstage during the last set, but she had disappeared by the time his stint was over. Grabbing his bag, he headed off to the beach hoping she was there. And she was.

"Hey." He ran the last few metres to her and swept her off her feet. His tongue delved and her legs wrapped around him. They barely made it a few paces before falling onto the sand where he plunged into her and had his way.

"Ugh, God, Pedro," she groaned as he rode her. "Oh, God."

It was over, and he was picking her up and taking her out to the platform where they rested. "Oh, God, that was good." He sighed.

She sat on top of him. "Was it good because it was sex with me or because you're high on drugs?"

His grin faltered. "What? I don't do drugs."

"Well…you do. Magnus put it in your drink."

He pushed her aside and sat up. "What?" he demanded angrily. "He put drugs in my drink? What the fuck!" He ran a hand through his hair. "What the fuck would he do that for?"

"My father's orders." She shrugged.

"Your father?" Pedro looked at her. "Who's your father?"

"Andros Poulos," she said simply.

Pedro stared. "What?" exploded out of him. "Andros Poulos is your father? Fucking hell. Why didn't you tell me? Fuck! I've been fucking my boss's daughter."

"I do have a mind and body of my own you know. I can do what I want."

"Are you even *old* enough to do what you want?"

"I'm eighteen." She tossed her hair over her shoulder. "And you're twenty, so it's only two years' difference."

"But you're my boss's daughter," he stressed. "Fuck."

"And Daddy's got his henchmen putting drugs in your drink. I saw him when I was there."

"Did he see you?"

"Nope. I hid behind the curtain."

"Fuck." Pedro rested his elbow on his bent knee and his head in his hand. "Fuck."

"Yes, we did, and you're very good at it."

He looked at her. "And we shouldn't be doing it. What if your father found out? He'd kill me."

"He probably would."

"He's already threatened to force me to work seven days. He pretended to rip my contract up the other day."

"You do know what my father does, right?" she asked curiously.

"Runs clubs."

"And guns and prostitutes and drugs."

Pedro frowned. "And now he's putting drugs in my drink. That's not on. Not on at all." He rubbed his forehead. "No wonder I've had headaches every day. I thought I was coming down with something."

"Nope. Just coming down from a drug-fuelled high."

"Do you know what an arsehole your father is?"

"Yep. He doesn't want me going to Juilliard in the fall."

Pedro's brows flew up. "You're a musician?"

"Classic piano and violin," she said. "I won my way in I was that good."

"And you're going to New York?" An idea formed in his mind.

"Yep. I'm going next month so I have a month to settle in before school. I wanted to get my fill of Greek island life before I went."

"I heard there was a new club opening there…"

"You should go. You're very good, and with your looks, everyone would want you."

"Think so?"

"Know so!"

Pedro agreed. "Definitely an idea. It's not as though Carlos is here anymore."

"I heard about that. I'm sorry."

He sighed. "Yeah, so am I. I can't find anything out. The cops wouldn't tell me. No one knows where he is."

"You'll find him."

"I hope so." He looked at his watch. "I gotta go." They swam back to the beach and got their belongings. "Will you be here tomorrow?" he asked, slipping on his shirt.

"I'll be waiting right here."

"See you then." He kissed her and wandered off.

She had watched them, hiding behind a stone pillar. The whore and Pedro. *Who the fuck does she think she is messing with my man?* She'd seen them fuck on the sand. Had only been a few paces from them, and had wanted to rip the whore's hair out. Had watched Pedro thrust into her with the magnificence of a stallion and then watched as he carried her to the water to swim to the platform where they'd talked. This was the second time she'd seen them together. The first was the other night after the club when she'd followed Pedro down to the beach and saw them fuck on the platform. She watched the girl walk down the cobblestone path and followed her all the way home where she climbed up the vines to a balcony and slid open French doors.

She took a few photos and vowed to find out who lived there.

*****

The next night, Pedro took a bag full of bottled water and juice from home. He substituted every bottle that Mikos or Magnus brought him and dumped it down the small sink backstage. They thought he was drinking it, but he was drinking his own. He felt good. Not high like previous nights, but as good as he had been. His headache was gone, he was feeling fit, and he partied until it was time to go home with Andros none the wiser.

He met Angelina at the beach, and they swam out to the platform where they made love. "Ah." Pedro rolled off her and she snuggled into his chest. "I'm not high, and that was even better."

"And how did you manage that?"

"Took my own from home and tipped theirs down the sink."

"Good for you. Outsmarting my father."

"I don't know how long it will last, though," he said. "How long can I keep it up before someone finds out?"

"As long as you need to." She leant up on her elbow. "Is New York still a plan?"

He smiled. "It's getting more serious every day. I got money saved up, my passport, a bag already packed."

"You *are* serious!"

"Yeah." He thought about it. "I packed it last week just in case."

"In case of what?"

"In case I found Carlos, or in case your father thinks ripping up my contract will make me work seven days a week."

Angelina sighed. "He can be forceful at times. He locked me in my room when I was sixteen. I had been sneaking out, and he found out, so he locked me in. It didn't last long. I got out and he realised I was too much like him to contain, so he let me set my own limits.

"How'd that work out?"

"I won a scholarship to Juilliard. How do you think it worked out?"

"Well, apparently." He kissed her, and she laid her head on his chest. "I should go soon. Gotta get home, and I bet you do too."

"Not yet," she said, leaving kisses down his stomach. She enveloped his member whole and delighted him with her prowess.

"Wow." He sighed. "Clearly I'm not your first."

"Clearly, I'm not yours, either," she replied.

"Nope."

"I think I should name it. Do you have a name for it?" She sucked some more.

"A name for what? My penis?" Pedro laughed.

"Yes."

"You're kidding, right?" His watch beeped, and he grabbed her and rolled off the platform into the water. They came up for air. "Time to go." They slowly swam for the shore and dressed. "See you tomorrow?"

"Same time, same place," she said, kissing him and watching him walk away. Once he was out of her line of vision, she headed for home and was on her way down a quiet road when she heard footsteps behind her. She slowed for a few moments then turned to fake out the stalker behind her, running smack bang into a woman with dark hair. "Oh, sorry. I didn't realise you were so close."

The woman stumbled back in shock.

"Here, let me help you." Angelina held out her hand.

The woman snarled. "Don't offer your hand to me, whore." She swung at Angelina with a clenched fist, but Angelina blocked her attempt with a quick spin kick.

The woman was down and clutching her stomach.

"You whore," she rasped from the ground.

"I have no idea who you are or why you're calling me a whore, but if you come near me again, I will do worse than that." Angelina flicked her hair over her shoulder and went on her way.

"You whore," the woman screamed. "Stay away from him, he's mine. Stay away from him." She groaned in pain. "The baby…the baby…"

July 1977

Pedro kept an eye out on Saturday night. Andros had come down to talk to him before the show asking how he was, how he was feeling.

"Great," he'd said. "Better than ever."

"Fantastic," Andros had replied. "Mikos, keep the juice flowing all night."

And that was it. Pedro made sure that every bottle of juice went down the small sink in his backstage area, or down the toilet when he pretended to be peeing.

He danced around the stage, imagining himself in New York, in a club with a different crowd. A crowd full of rich men and richer women. Women who wanted him and him alone. Screaming for him, reaching for him, ripping his clothes off and taking him into their mouths.

Oh, how he wanted that.

He decided there and then if he lasted the summer in Santorini he'd be ready for the bright lights of New

York City come September. He finished off the night and thanked everyone for coming. Backstage he towelled down and grabbed his bag.

"Pedro." Andros came through the door. "Great show my boy, how do you feel?"

Not this again!

"Fine, Mr Poulos." He high-fived the part-time DJ who took care of the beats in the wee hours and shut everything down and packed it away for him. "Why do you keep asking?"

"Just wondering," Andros said. "I'm having a big party here next week. A going away party for my daughter and her friends. I was wondering if you would DJ. I'll pay you your going rate, of course. It will be Wednesday night. I know you don't normally work that night."

"I'll let you know tomorrow." Pedro hefted his bag onto his shoulder. "I'll have to check to see if I have anything else on. Is that all?"

"Yes, yes, of course," Andros said. "Have a good night. And have a good sleep. You'll be doing this all again tomorrow night."

"I will. Bye." Pedro was out the door and heading for the beach. He met Angelina there and all but dragged her out to the platform. "Did you know your father's throwing you a going away party at the club next Wednesday? He asked me to DJ for it. Oh, God, what are you doing…?"

Her head lifted from his groin. "Getting your microphone warmed up."

"My what?" He laughed. "My microphone? Is that

what you're calling it?"

"For now." She grinned. "I'm coming up with different names to see what suits it most. Figured I'd go for a musical theme for a name. Are you warmed up yet?"

"For what?" he teased.

"This," she replied and mounted him.

"Oh, God." He threw his arms out and lay back on the platform as she worked her way up and down. The slick wetness, the warmth, the sweet, sweet motherlode.

"So, are you going to do it?"

"Ugh, huh?" He came to. "Do what?"

"DJ at my party."

His eyes slowly opened and he focussed on her face. "You want me to? What if he realises we know each other?"

"How could he? I don't go to the club, so it's not as if I would have met you anywhere else." She slid up and down.

"And how will we keep our hands off each other?" He slid his hands up her thighs to her hips and onto her breasts, and she held them there as she moved.

"Who said we have to?" She clenched, and he groaned. "I'm sure I could slip backstage and you could slip inside during a break. It will be over in a flash, and I'll be back at the party before Daddy even sees I'm gone."

"And what if he does see that you're gone, and I'm gone, and we're gone together?" He thrust up into her.

"Ahhhh." She sucked in air. "Then I'll say," she

mumbled. "I was thanking you for being the DJ at my party." She sighed. "That was good."

He breathed deeply as she collapsed onto him. "Yes, it was."

She stroked his arm slowly, her head on his chest, her ear above his heart. The stars overhead blanketed them, and she heard the beating of solitude. Stretching, she clenched around him and relaxed fully.

"So, what do we do?"

"Nothing. Pretend we've just met and I'm thanking you for playing my party, nothing more." She looked up into his eyes. "Don't worry."

"Easy for you to say," he said.

*****

Wednesday night the party started at seven.

Pedro was behind his deck, Angelina and all of her friends on the dance floor, and Andros on stage embarrassing his daughter.

"We are here tonight to say farewell to my little girl, Angelina."

Her friends cheered, and Pedro saw her go red. As red as the hot lace dress she had on. The same dress he'd first fucked her in, except this time she had a slip under it.

"She has worked her little Greek butt off to get into one of the most prestigious music colleges of all time, and now she is flying off to New York, on the other side of the world. Away from her papa, her friends, her family. So tonight we say goodbye to my little

Angelina." Her friends cheered once more and closed around her.

Andros waved at Pedro who started the music and got the crowds moving for the next eight hours.

At three in the morning things slowed down. Pedro was out the back in the alley taking a break, and Angelina managed to sneak out to see him. She flew into his arms, and he spun her around.

"We have to be careful. What if your father sees us, or Magnus, or Mikos, or anyone else?"

She smothered him in kisses. "I don't care. I am *so* happy. That was so good." She kissed him. "Fuck me."

Shock flew over his face. "What? Here? Someone will see." There was a sound at the back door and Pedro saw movement. "Someone *did* see. You'd better go."

"No. I don't care," she said defiantly.

He put her down. "Go. I don't need trouble from your father. Go."

"Pedro," she said. "He *won't* find out."

"Pedro!" bellowed through the back of the club and out the door.

"He already did. Go, go," he whispered, and she ran down the alley.

Andros burst out the door. "Where is my daughter? What are you doing with my daughter?"

"Your daughter?" Pedro frowned. "Your daughter's not here." He put his hands out and looked around. "I'm just having a break."

"My daughter *was* here." He barged over to Pedro, got him by the shirt, and hauled him up against the wall. "I know my daughter was here and that the two of you were kissing."

"I wasn't doing any such thing." Pedro put his hands up. "I haven't touched your daughter."

"Magnus saw you, heard you, heard her ask you to fuck her," he spat, and droplets flew onto Pedro who frowned and turned away. "If you lay one hand on my daughter I will kill you."

"I haven't touched your daughter," Pedro muttered through clenched teeth. Andros's face was in his, and he was feeling the panic rise.

Angelina was hiding behind some trash cans and had seen and heard everything her father said and did, and she didn't like it one bit. Gripping a lid, she sneaked along the wall, came up behind her father, and smacked him hard on the back of the head.

Andros Poulos dropped like a lead balloon.

Pedro stood plastered against the wall, gasping for air as Angelina stood in the middle of the alley holding the can lid.

"What the fuck did you do?" Pedro whispered loudly.

Angelina had a big grin on her face. "Oh, something I've wanted to do for a very long time," she gushed.

The door burst open and Magnus came barging out. "Mr Poulos, Angelina." He flew to Angelina's side. "What did this man do to you?" He started toward Pedro, but Angelina cracked him on the back of the head with the lid. Magnus fell like a tonne of bricks onto his boss.

"This is crazy," Pedro cried hoarsely. "What are you

doing?" He looked down at the two men at his feet. "You're crazy if you think you can get away with it. What the fuck are you doing?"

"Giving us a head start." She dropped the lid onto the men. "Get your stuff, and let's go."

"Go where?" He looked at her in a daze.

"To my place. Come on, get your bag." But when Pedro just stood there staring at her, she ran inside, snatched his bag from backstage, ran back out, and grabbed him by the hand. "Let's go."

They took off through the winding streets of Santorini until they reached her house. She climbed the trellis and went into her room, hauling two suitcases onto the balcony. "Here, catch." She dropped one at a time down to Pedro and then went in for two small bags which went the same way over the balcony. She put her carry-on bag and handbag over her head and grabbed her violin case. After climbing back down, she adjusted her bags. "Let's get to the wharf. We can take a plane to Mykonos for your stuff and then fly to Athens for the airport."

"What?" Pedro was still in shock. "This is crazy."

"Come on." She ushered him down to the wharf where the family seaplane was and got the pilot to kick start it into life. "Mykonos and step on it." She crammed her bags and cases into the small plane, and fifteen minutes later they landed in Mykonos. She hurried Pedro to his home, and he quietly went in and got his case and bag. Leaving a quick note for his parents on his mother's bedside table, he kissed her on the cheek and left as quietly as he'd come.

They raced back to the wharf and added his luggage to Angelina's.

"Athens, and step on it," she told the pilot.

A half hour later, they landed at the dock and loaded a taxi. "Thank you," she told the pilot. "Spend the night in Athens on me." She shoved money into the man's hand. "Go and have a drink or three."

He nodded his thanks and grabbed the next taxi.

"What was that for?" Pedro whispered in the back of their cab.

"If he's out of action my father can't find him, or us," she whispered back.

They got to the airport and Angelina paid the driver handsomely. "Take the night off," she said, and he doffed his cap.

Gathering their bags and cases, they rolled in to buy some tickets. There was a wait of thirty minutes on the plane to New York, and they quickly sent their luggage off and went to wait at the boarding gate.

"This is crazy." Pedro pulled her to a quiet place. "They're probably awake by now and calling the cops if they didn't half an hour ago."

Angelina looked at her watch. "Father was probably out for most of the time, and then he would have sent his goons looking for me and you in Santorini first. He would have asked my friends if they'd seen me or knew where I was. He'd be sending someone to check your parents' place, and he probably would have found out that our seaplane has gone. But he won't think we have completely gone unless he realises my luggage is."

"And then he'll know we're here and we have another," he checked his watch, "twenty minutes to go."

"He won't know until it's too late." She dug around in her bag and pulled out a scarf which she wrapped around her hair, completely covering it in a bun. She slid a sleeveless lightweight kimono jacket over her dress and tied it up. "There, that's me." She looked at Pedro. "Change your top and put a cap on."

With a shake of his head, he dug into his carry-on and changed his shirt, much to the delight of the women in the area, and pulled on an old baseball cap.

"Flight 333 from Athens to New York City is now boarding. Flight 333 from Athens to New York City is now boarding."

"That's us, let's go," she said, and dragged him through the boarding gate and onto the plane.

The next fifteen minutes for final boarding and then the ten minutes on the tarmac were hell for Pedro, whose stomach remained clenched the whole time. It wasn't until he was in the air that he relaxed. He was headed for New York City and a crack at international stardom.

*****

Two days later, Pedro stepped out of the brownstone in Gramercy and stood on the street. He breathed deeply; still not believing he was in New York. Life had been a whirlwind since leaving Greece, and they'd hidden with Maggie, a friend of Angelina's, who was going to Juilliard as well.

Her parents were away for the rest of the summer, and she had the place to herself. They had gone there straight from the airport, and with one look at Pedro, Maggie was saying yes to everything. Yes, to them hiding out there. Yes, to not telling Angelina's father she had seen them. Yes, to anything Pedro asked for, and he'd asked for a map of the city and raided the phone book for a list of all the clubs. He wanted to get started job hunting right away, but Angelina had other ideas.

"Shouldn't we lie low for a while?" Angelina had *purred in his ear the night before. "My father will be after us."*

"You've changed your tune from two days ago," he'd said. *"But no. I'm here. I want to work, it's what I love."*

"Well, you're what I love," she'd murmured and *slid her mouth around him.*

Now he was ready to hit the streets for a job. Having heard about a hot new club that would be opening soon, he decided to start there and set out for 254 West and 54th Streets, finding the building work still going on outside. He stopped a worker and asked where he could find the owner or manager and was directed inside. Pedro walked into a spacious club with disco dance floor, stage and DJ booth, tables, and groups of people running around testing everything.

"I want the lights to go there, there and there," a man was yelling.

"Excuse me, I want to audition for the DJ position," Pedro said to him.

"It's already taken." The man glanced at him and did a double take. He eagerly eyed the hot-looking guy in front of him, but the clothes turned him off. "Position's already filled, kid." He turned away.

Pedro scoured the room, saw some people looking at him, and did what he did best. He dropped his bag and ripped his shirt off. "How 'bout now?"

The man looked back and didn't stop looking at the beautiful Greek god before him. The jet-black hair and bright blue eyes would be an attraction and so would that body. "What job did you say you wanted?"

"DJ. I've been DJing in the Greek Islands for two years."

The man eagerly nodded. "It looks like it. Get up on stage and show us what you got." He nodded to the DJ booth.

Pedro smiled his charming smile. "Give me a minute to pick something out." He walked past his admirers, dropped his bag and shirt beside the booth, picked a couple of records and donned the headphones. Within seconds he was mixing the tracks, scratching the sounds, and making sweet music to the crowd of onlookers. He danced, he sang, he moved to the music and went on until the songs were done. He removed the headphones. "I get the job?" he called down to the guy.

"Yep, kid." The man broke into applause, and the rest of the room followed. "You get the job."

Pedro collected his things, went over to the man and shook his hand. "Knew you couldn't resist me."

The man raised a brow. "With a body like that *no*

one will be able to resist you. Go and see Stew about the payroll and get yourself signed up. You'll get a thousand a week."

"A bit of a downgrade from my last job, but I'll cope with it," Pedro joked.

"What were you earning on your last job?" The man wondered if he fucked women for money. Or men. *Wouldn't mind trying that out myself,* he thought.

"A thousand a night."

The man eyed the smooth, creamy skin and hair-free chest. "You're definitely worth a thousand a night." *Oh, yes,* he thought, *I'd pay that for five minutes with you.* "Stew," he yelled, and a man came scurrying over. "Get this kid on the payroll for a thousand a night. He's our new DJ."

Stew eyed Pedro. "Sure, come with me."

Pedro shook the man's hand. "I didn't catch your name," he said.

"Eddie. Eddie Monteif."

"Well, thanks for the opportunity, Eddie, I won't let you down."

"Oh, I know you won't, kid. I know you won't."

Pedro started following Stew, but stopped and turned around. "What's the name of the place going to be so I know where to tell my friends to go?"

"*Studio 69,* kid. *Studio 69.*"

*****

A week later, Pedro was laying down the tracks on the

opening night of *Studio 69.* He was dancing behind the deck wearing nothing but short shorts, which didn't worry him after wearing not much more growing up on Mykonos and DJing in next to nothing. He did a double spin and waved his arms in the air getting cheers and whoops from the crowd.

While the atmosphere was the same, the essence was different. This was stylish, upper class and rich. It *was* New York after all. Rich women paraded past him on the floor, and so did the men. He saw celebrities from his favourite TV shows and movies, singers, musicians and bands. They were the high social elite of the city and they all stopped to look at him, the hot new DJ in the hot new club.

There had been no word from Andros, not that that meant anything. He could be waiting to make a move, but Pedro would deal with it when it came.

Angelina was down in the crowd thrusting her hips left, right and centre. She was with Maggie and a few other friends.

Waiters in short shorts roller-skated around dealing out drinks and anything else people wanted. It was electric. The atmosphere was filled with heat and sweat and lust and sex. It was so electrifying that Pedro was glad to be a part of it.

Ten hours later he finished up as the doors closed in the early hours of the morning. Angelina and Maggie had gone home, stragglers had lingered, and now the club was being cleaned up.

"Hey, kid," Eddie called out. "Great job tonight. Worth every cent you are." He was puffing on a cigar and sitting with a group of men Pedro didn't know.

"Thanks, Mr Monteif." Pedro pulled a t-shirt on to a loud round of boos. "Not the first time I've had that happen." He laughed and went to the staff room and changed out of his shorts.

Mike Gatos, one of the bartenders, came in. "You were great up there. How long have you been DJing?" He threw a t-shirt over his head.

"Two years," Pedro replied. "The summers are big on Mykonos and Santorini."

"Yeah, I've heard." Mike stepped out of his shorts. "You wanna go play some more? I find that I can't wind down for a couple of hours." He pulled a pair of jeans on. "Takes me a while to get to sleep."

"No, thanks." Pedro stood and threw his bag over his shoulder. "Got a girl waiting."

"Lucky you. That hot little number in the red dress?"

"Yep."

"Lucky bastard." Mike threw a rolled up towel at him.

Pedro laughed and ducked. "That's what everyone says. Night."

"Night."

Pedro walked outside and hailed a cab. Getting back to Gramercy in half an hour, he was showered and by Angelina's side.

*****

The woman walked back to her flimsy hotel room and

cranked the air con. It was hot, stuffy, and she was too damn sweaty. How the hell did Pedro put up with it? Pulling the latest pack of developed pictures from her bag, she eagerly pored through them and picked out the best three, pinning them to the large corkboard on the desk, alongside all the other pictures of Pedro and a few of Carlos that she'd managed to take before he shot through. She stroked Pedro's face in her favourite photo. He was standing on the beach naked and on full display. Her tongue peeked out to lick her lips. She'd always tried to do it seductively, practising in the mirror for hours, but it never came across that way. She just looked like a girl licking her lips.

Her finger headed down from his face to his manhood. Oh, how she loved his appendage and would love to measure it, feel it in her hand again, feel it inside of her. She nearly had once, but he'd pushed her away. He had been scared, she understood that. They'd never made love before, and she had come off as a bit pushy. But he'd soon see how wonderful she could be. More womanly, more adult, more than that whore he was sleeping with. Who the fuck did that little tramp think she was to be taking her man. And doing her karate shit…the bitch had kicked her in the stomach.

"The baby, my baby, our baby," she murmured at the picture of Pedro. "Our baby." She stroked his penis and saw it grow, saw it rise. It was bigger than Carlos's, he was only ten inches, while Pedro packed an extra inch, and oh how that extra inch would come in handy. Oh, how it would fill her so. Fill her to every inch of her body and make her come with such pleasure. So much more than Carlos. He was good, but Pedro was better. And he would soon be hers.

She collected the photos of Pedro and Angelina together in New York and on Santorini, fucking each other. She put them in an envelope and sealed it tight. It was already addressed to Andros Poulos care of SantorPoulos in Santorini. "Oh, yes, whore, I will get rid of you. Daddy's going to know exactly where you are and who you're with." Screwing up the excess photos, she threw them into the rubbish bin where they landed next to the empty box of red hair dye.

September 1977

"Won't your father know you've started classes?" Pedro asked the morning of Angelina's start at Juilliard.

She shrugged. "Probably, if he has someone watching the school, or if he can be bothered making the call. They'll probably just write and tell him." She dressed for her first day in a pretty summer dress and cardigan. It may have been the start of fall, but it was still hitting the high 80s.

"What if he comes here?" Pedro hadn't even been to sleep yet having gotten home from the club as she was getting up at 6:30.

"Then we'll deal with it," she said and grabbed her bag. "Wish me luck." She stuck out her lips for a kiss.

"Good luck." He gave her what she wanted and slept the rest of the day until he strode through the back door of the club at six. He'd been there just over a month, and it still felt amazing. September in New York was beautiful. Angelina was beautiful. Life was beautiful, and Pedro knew he had it all. All he'd ever want to do. DJ in one of the hottest clubs in the world and *Studio 69* was just that. It had become the hottest place to be, to be *seen* in, and he was a part of that.

"Hey, Pedro, what's up, man?" Mike walked into the staff room after him.

"Hey, man, nothing much." Pedro pulled his t-shirt off and unzipped his jeans.

"I hear some bigwig producers are coming in tonight," Mike said.

"Music producers?" Pedro slid into his shorts.

"Nah, man, *movie* producers." Mike pulled up his own shorts; short, gold and tight.

"What sort of movies?" Leon, a roller-skating bartender asked as he came through the door. "Big screen movies?" He fluttered his false eyelashes and did a twirl. "I could be in movies. Don't I have the face for it?" He held his hands under his face to frame it. Leon was a gay black man who talked as flamboyantly as he walked, *and* dressed. Today he was wearing a tight crop top, even tighter leopard print pants, platform boots, and a pink feather boa.

"Hey, Leon." Pedro smiled indulgently, pretending he hadn't heard it all before. "I didn't know you wanted to be in movies. You never said anything."

"Oh, darling," Leon's New York accent came thick and fast as he sat beside Pedro, crossed his legs, and clasped his hands together on his knee. "Let me tell you about the time—"

"Enough already," Mike said. "We've heard it a million times, and we've only been working here for six weeks."

"Well, make it a million and one then," Leon replied before being cut off by Richard, the staff manager.

"Eddie wants you all out on the main floor for a little chat before we open."

"We'll be there in a minute," Pedro told him, and Richard retreated.

"How could that poor man's mother call him Richard," Leon said as he fussed around in his locker.

"What do you mean?" Mike asked.

"Well, their surname is Head, don't ya know," Leon replied. "And his name is Richard. She clearly didn't think about that one."

Mike and Pedro shrugged at each other. They had no idea what Leon was talking about.

"Oh, for heaven's sake." Leon rolled his eyes. "His name is Richard Head. The nickname for Richard is Dick." Leon spread his hands. "His name is Dick Head."

Pedro and Mike snorted. "Get out," Pedro said and grabbed his bag. They walked out to the main floor and waited for Eddie to talk.

"Boys," he called. "We've got some very special people coming tonight. They'll be my guests for the evening, so they are to be treated very well indeed. Whatever they want, whatever they need, we will supply it. You got that?"

"Yes, sir!"

"Good boys," Eddie said. "The other thing is that they are big time movie producers and are on the lookout for new talent."

"Ooohhh, that's me, that's me." Leon waved and twirled around.

Eddie sighed. "It could be any of you, all of you, one of you, none of you. So be on your best behaviour and give them what you've got. Right?"

"Yes, sir!"

"Right, now let's get ready for tonight." He clapped his hands and the staff went their separate ways.

Pedro stepped behind his deck and booted up the system. He always came alive when he got behind his booth and set the needle on the records. It filled him like nothing else ever did.

Not even Angelina.

People started piling into the club and headed straight for him. He had the same fans every night; socialites in their thirties, gay men in their twenties. Every night they were first in the door, they stood in front of his booth all night, and were the last out the door.

He waved to Bev Marie, the high-end fashion model, and threw a cheeky grin at Sara Holdare, the CEO of a hot cosmetics company who became a millionaire by the age of thirty-eight. And that was three years ago. Now she was sitting on *tens* of millions and knew how to flash the cash.

Martine Krevnokov was in the crowd. The wife of a Russian oil baron made her life in New York while her husband lived with his mistress in St Petersburg. Her nickname was Ice Queen for the blondest of blonde hair and bluest of blue eyes. The silver sable fur coat seemed out of place for September considering that summer was hanging on. She was dressed in a skin-tight silver jumpsuit that showed there was no way anything was underneath it, and silver glittered heels so high Pedro wondered how she didn't fall. Or break an ankle.

Stan Kosnov was beside her dancing as though his life depended on it. He was a business man by day, dancer out of the closet by night, and he'd taken a shine to Pedro.

Pedro danced behind his console, waving his hands at the crowd, getting them screaming and singing.

"I told you the kid was good," Eddie told his guests.

"He's gorgeous," a woman said, and the others agreed. "But quite a few of them are good looking." She was Greta Von Burro, American born, and of Swedish descent. Her parents had been refugees after the war. She'd grown up in Chicago, Illinois, but resided full-time in New York.

"I like the bartender," a man in his late thirties said. He was Thomas Derbon, publicity and management. He'd been out of the closet for two years and had no problems telling people that.

"Which one?" Greta asked.

"The brunet with the smattering of hair… Ohhh." He shivered delicately. "I love chest hair…delicious."

"Well, take your pick," Eddie told them. "Whichever one you want."

"Stephanie," Greta said to the brunette woman with her. "What do you think?"

Stephanie Martison was a forty-something director and producer who loved men and loved cocks even more. "Definitely the DJ. Look at him. Tall, dark, handsome, gorgeous, dances, DJs. I wonder if he sings." She sipped her champagne. "I definitely wouldn't mind trying him out."

"*You* would," Greta said. "Carson, what about you?"

"Considering Harry's latest acquisition, we need someone outstanding. Someone who's going to make the girls crazy and make the men want to be him." Carson Trumack was a forty-something star-maker. Everyone he'd picked had been a winner.

"Yes," Greta said, looking in Pedro's direction. "He *is* gorgeous."

The woman entered the club and made her way to the centre of the dance floor. She watched Pedro spinning and dancing on stage and saw all of the people gathered in front of him. The one she didn't see was Angelina. The whore wasn't there to support her man. Why would she be when schooling was more important? *I'll slash the bitch's face,* she thought viciously, but quickly calmed down. She was bumped from behind. "Hey, watch it," she snapped at one of the roller-skating waiters.

"Sorry," Leon called and rolled away.

She went back to watching Pedro.

Down the front, Bev and Sara were trying to carry on a conversation.

"I wonder if he's single." Bev adjusted the bosom of her dress to show more cleavage. "And I mean single single, not single but dating."

"Would it be a problem if he was?" Martine joined

in. The ladies knew each other from social engagements, but weren't friends. "Look at my husband, Sergei. I am here, he is with mistress."

"Not everyone willingly cheats on his girlfriend or wife," Sara told her.

"No." Martine slithered up and down. "But many do. And many don't care."

Over on the sidelines, Stephanie was intently watching. "Look at the way he has these women eating out of his hand," she said. "They're almost lining up to be with him, to be picked *by* him."

"I'd love to be picked by him." Thomas sipped his drink.

"He has them lined up against the stage every night," Eddie said. "He's been our most popular staff member."

"How much do you pay him?" Greta asked.

"A thousand a night."

"Oh, he's worth so much more than that," she replied.

Down in the crowd, the woman made her way through it, not taking her eyes off Pedro. She came to a stop behind the three women whoring themselves at the stage and listened while they stared adoringly up at him.

"Does it really matter if he's single?" Bev asked. "I wanna fuck him anyway."

"I wonder how big his penis is," Martine added.

"I'd love to get my tongue in that mouth," Sara said.

"I'd love to get my mouth around his cock," Bev interjected.

"You whores," the woman spat. "You can't keep your legs together or your mouths shut, you always have to go after other women's men. You're all a pack of fucking whores."

"And what the fuck are you?" Martine asked. She was Russian bred all the way. "What business is it of yours what we do?" Eyeing the little red-haired girl with the mousy complexion and plain figure, she said, "Run along little girl, you're not wanted here." She clicked her fingers at a waiter. "Get security, this girl is harassing us."

The waiter rolled away.

"Time to go, little girl," Martine told her.

The commotion that came next was heard through the whole club, and everyone stopped and stared as Martine Krevnokov got the red-haired girl into a headlock after she had tried to claw her eyes out. Bev and Sara stood back laughing as security removed the woman from Martine's Russian Ice Queen grip.

Pedro saw the whole thing go down and kept the beats going as security dragged the woman away. The woman looked vaguely familiar, but he couldn't place her. Half an hour later, while on his break, he was called over to Eddie's table.

"Hey, kid, I want you to meet Greta, Stephanie, Thomas and Carson; they're the producers I told you all about."

Pedro nodded his greetings. "Nice to meet you. Enjoying yourselves?"

All four eyed off Pedro's body. Six feet of rock-hard deliciousness topped off with a chiselled jaw, straight white teeth, and big blue eyes.

"You ever thought of acting, kid?" Eddie asked.

Pedro shrugged. "Who hasn't?"

"We're not talking about *normal* acting, though," Greta said. She leant toward him in her seat. "We're talking movies…porn movies."

Pedro frowned. "Then nope, not interested," he said with a brief shake of his head.

"But look at you, you're gorgeous, and if I may be bold, I bet you've got a big cock," Greta followed up.

Pedro's frown deepened and his hands went to his hips. "Excuse me?"

"Here, take a look at Harry DeVille's latest acquisition." Carson pulled a photo from a folder. "He's gorgeous, but I bet you'll make a million more."

Pedro took the 8x10 photo and looked at the guy in it. Recognition dawned and his brows flew to his hairline. "Oh, my God, Carlos…"

"You know Carlo Stefan?" Four voices asked him.

Pedro looked up in confusion. "Who? Carlo Stefan? No, no, this is Carlos Stephanopoulos, my brother."

"Jesus Fucking Christ," the four of them said at once.

"Carlo is your brother?" Greta asked, barely daring to believe what this could mean.

Pedro huffed. "Ah, yeah!" He looked at his brother standing in a replica of the cabana he worked in. It was all Carlos. "Where was this taken? *When* was it taken?"

"Last week for his upcoming debut in one of the hottest porn movies ever released. It's a publicity shot for the movie," Thomas told him. "Are you *sure* he's your brother? You look nothing alike."

Pedro looked up from the photo. "He's older than me by four years and takes after Mama who's Australian. Our brother Tomas looks exactly like Papa, and I take after both. So yeah, this is definitely Carlos. Where is he, do you know? I haven't seen him since June on Mykonos."

"He's in Hollywood," Greta replied. "Harry DeVille is a huge go-getter in the business and he got your brother. So…" Standing, she walked around him. "How about making yourself *our* latest acquisition?" Staring up into his eyes she was mesmerised. "We could do so much with you, Pedro Stephanopoulos." She melted into the floor.

Pedro glanced from her to the others, seeing them all eagerly waiting for his reply, to the photo in his hand. *Carlos…a porn star?* "I don't know," he finally said, looking at his watch. "My break is nearly over. Can I keep this?" He waved the picture. "I need to think this over."

"Of course," Greta slid her fingers over his hand. "I'll leave our details with Eddie for you to pick up later. I look forward to hearing from you."

"Uh, yeah." Pedro backed away and all but ran for the stage.

"We need him." Thomas stood beside her. "He's the brother of Harry's latest stud. *Can you believe the coup?* We *need* him. *I* need him." Thomas licked his lips. "God how I need him."

"Keep it in your pants, Tommy boy," Greta told

him. "He's reluctant. Didn't you see the look on his face when he realised it was his brother? Something is definitely going on here. He didn't even know where his brother was. I wonder what the story is."

Stephanie moved closer to them. "And did you hear what he said? There's *another brother.* God, if he looks like those two then whoever scores him won't know what hit them."

"I'd like to see all three up close and in person." Carson joined them. "*And* in a movie together. Imagine it!"

In unison they tilted their heads, imagining Pedro, Carlos and the other brother in a porno together.

"We could call it *Porn Star Brothers,*" Thomas murmured, imagining his mouth sliding around cocks so big. "Carlos is ten inches. I wonder what Pedro is."

"Yours if you want him," Eddie yelled from his seat.

They turned and took their seats.

"*Can* we have him?" Greta sat by Eddie and laid her hand on his. *"We want him."*

"Well," Eddie drawled. "He's still mine by night during the week...but what he does during the day and on the weekend is up to him. Think you can work around that?"

"Oh." Greta smiled. "Absolutely."

Pedro finished off for the night and headed for the staff room. He was changing when Mike and Leon walked in.

"Whoo, dude! Did I see you talking to those bigwigs with Eddie?" Mike asked.

Pedro gave a half grin. "Yeah." He pulled his pants on.

"And did they want you to star in their latest movie?" Leon flapped around him. "The Greek God of *Studio 69*."

Pedro made a face. "Yeah."

Leon and Mike stared.

"They what?" Mike asked.

"They want you for their movie." Leon stared, wide-eyed.

"Yeah." Pedro put his stuff away.

"Oh, my God," Leon squealed. "We've got the next big movie star on our hands." He started dancing.

"Except it's not a normal movie," Pedro said.

Leon stopped. "What do you mean…*not a normal movie?*"

A guttural noise came from Pedro's throat and he looked up at the ceiling. "Ugh, they want me for pornos."

Silence.

"Oh, my God, you're kidding," Leon screamed and jumped up and down. "They want you for pornos. Oh, my God. You have to do it. Look at you." He eyed Pedro up and down. "You have *got* to do it. You'd make a gazillion dollars."

"No." Pedro shook his head. "I don't know if I want to be in a porno. It's bad enough my brother is, and I've only just found out after three months of not knowing where he was or what he was doing."

"Wait…what…?" Leon stopped him. "Your *brother* is in pornos." He exchanged glances with Mike. "You didn't tell *me* you had a brother." He playfully slapped Pedro's arm. "Do you have a picture?"

Pedro dug the 8x10 out of his bag and handed it over. "I just found out tonight that he's in L.A. doing pornos."

Leon took the photo and his eyes grew to the size of saucers. Mike leant over his shoulder. "Oh, child," Leon said. "Mmm, mmm, mmm, mmm, mmm. What a tasty morsel your brother is." He peered closer. "Is that ten inches?"

Pedro snatched it back. "All right, enough, thank you." He glanced at the photo and put it in his bag. "I have no idea what Mama and Papa are going to say when they see this."

"They don't know?" Mike asked, zipping up his bag.

"I don't know," Pedro replied. "I haven't spoken to them since I left in July."

"Time to call your folks and tell them." Leon threw an animal print fur coat around his shoulders and adjusted a matching hat on his head. "I'm off darlings, to get *my* fill of ten inches somewhere else since I can't have your brother." He flounced out the door then stopped. "By the way…if he's ten inches, how big are you?"

"Get out." Pedro pointed at the door.

Eddie walked in after Leon walked out. "Here's Greta's details for you. She said to call her if you're interested."

Pedro took the business card and looked at it. *Greta Von Burro, Adult Movie Producer, 555-6567.* He sighed and threw it into his bag with the photo. "Thanks, Eddie."

"You're not sure about it are you, kid?" Eddie asked.

Pedro sat heavily on the bench in the middle of the room. "I think it was more the shock of finding my brother and seeing what he was doing than being asked if I'd do it too."

"You and your brother close?" Eddie asked, sitting next to him.

"We are…were. He took off in June and we haven't heard anything since."

"And when did you take off?"

"July." Pedro stared at him.

"Told your parents?"

He looked away. "No."

"Then how do you know he hasn't called them?"

Pedro sighed. "I don't."

"Then it's time to call your parents."

With a deep sigh, Pedro left and walked home to Angelina's apartment to find her getting ready for school. "You got a minute?"

"Can you tell me while I get ready?" She ran around their room grabbing her bag and shoes. "You can help me pick out a dress."

Pedro sat on the bed. "We had some big movie producers in last night and they offered me a lead role."

Her eyes lit up. "Wow, really? That's great. How about this one?" She held up a blue floral dress.

"No." Pedro shook his head at the choice.

"That's awesome," she continued. "What movie?"

"A porno."

Silence.

She turned from the closet. "A what-o?"

"A porno."

Walking over, she stood in front of him. "They want you to star in a porno?"

He nodded. "Yep."

Her mouth moved while she thought about what to say. "Ah, what, ah, did you tell them?"

He shrugged. "I said I needed to think about it."

She drew in a breath. "And what did you tell them that for?"

"Because of this." He pulled out the photo of Carlos.

She took it. "Ah, Carlo Stefan." Shaking her head, she went on. "Who's…?" Then she realised from seeing the look on his face.

"Ugh," Pedro muttered. "My brother's doing pornos."

"Ohhh," came out in a sigh. Angelina tucked a strand of hair behind her ear. "And they want you?"

Pedro got up and stood looking out the window of their tiny apartment. "Apparently, he's some bigwig's latest acquisition and they were looking for one for themselves to compete. They had no idea I knew him. When I mentioned it, they got all excited and all but begged me to be their new star." He shook his head. "I was so confused at seeing Carlos that I said I needed to think about it."

"Fair enough," Angelina said. "So, now what?"

"My boss suggested I call my parents since I haven't spoken to them since I left." He shrugged a shoulder. "He may have gotten in contact with them. I don't know."

"Then maybe it's time you did." She glanced at the clock. "Have a chat with your parents first. Don't worry about the porn stuff for now. You obviously need to get the Carlos thing sorted out." She threw on a pink dress and grabbed her bag. "I gotta go, I'll see you later." She kissed him. "I love you."

"I love you, too," he said and watched her leave. Sitting on the bed, biting his lip, he deliberated for twenty minutes before he called his parents.

The phone rang and rang… "Hello."

"Mama."

"Pedro…? Oh, my God, Pedro, my baby. Where are you, are you all right, what are you doing, why haven't you called or written, when are you coming home?"

"Mama, slow down. I'm okay. I'm more than okay. I'm awesome."

"Where are you?"

"I'm in New York."

Silence.

"New York? What are you doing there?"

Silence.

"I followed a friend over and got myself a job in a new club as a DJ. It's great, Mama. Everything I wanted. The club is famous, the people are famous. I get paid the same amount I did in Santorini."

"At Andros Poulos's place?"

Silence.

"Yeah."

"And this friend of yours…" pause, "…is Angelina Poulos…"

Silence.

"Yeah."

"He came to us, Pedro." Her voice rose. "He came to us and told us you had raped his daughter and assaulted him. Then the two of you disappeared. He was going to press charges and have you hunted down like a dog."

Silence.

Pedro frowned at the news. "I'm sorry, Mama, but I did no such thing. Angelina is eighteen and she's going to Juilliard. She's the one that hit him and helped me leave." He sighed. "Look, have you heard from Carlos?"

Silence.

"Yes. He called last month. He's in Hollywood doing okay. He's happy and healthy, and the charges against him have been dropped, apparently."

Pedro let out a whoosh of air. "That's good, oh, that's good to hear."

"Unlike you, Pedro. Have you spoken to him?"

"No. I didn't even know where he was."

"Do you know where Tomas is?"

He frowned again. "He's not there either?"

"No. He left to spread his wings not long after you, but that was his choice, not because he was in trouble. All of my babies have left me, and I didn't know where any of you were."

"Oh, Mama, it's okay. I'm in New York, and Carlos is in Hollywood. Making a name for himself in movies, I think."

"How do you know?"

Silence.

"I saw him in a publicity shot for a movie that's coming out soon."

Silence.

"Oh…he didn't say anything to me. Said he didn't want me to know too much in case someone tried getting information out of us."

Pedro nodded. "Wise move. The less you guys know, the better. What about Tomas? You haven't heard from him?"

"I haven't heard back since he left. I think he was going to America too. Miami, maybe. My babies have left me," she cried.

"Mama, Mama, don't cry," he soothed. "We're okay, we're alive."

"Not if Andros Poulos gets you."

"Well, he hasn't yet, and I'll deal with him if he does. I gotta go. I love you, Mama."

"I love you, Pedro, my baby. Call soon."

"I will. Bye."

*****

Andros Poulos sat behind his desk in his office at the club. He was pissed. Not only had Angelina taken off for New York, but she'd taken off with his stud DJ in tow. The stud DJ who'd been fucking her. He ripped open an envelope. Sales had been down since Pedro had gone, and while he wasn't paying out a thousand a night, he was losing more than that in tourists. No one wanted to come now Pedro was gone. And while the new DJ he'd hired was good, he didn't cut it the way Pedro did.

Pulling photos out of the envelope, he looked at

Angelina and Pedro on the streets of New York, in the club, and fucking on the beach. His hand shook with uncontrollable rage, and he screwed the photos into tiny balls. He'd been warned against seeking revenge upon Pedro, but now he would no longer heed that warning.

He knew Angelina was at Juilliard; he had called, but now knew Pedro was with her. He'd kept his distance by having a man watch his daughter, but he'd never seen Pedro with her. If he worked in a club, he'd be out all night and sleeping all day. No wonder he'd not been seen.

Andros now knew where he was and a plan started formulating. He was going to get Pedro Stephanopoulos if it was the last thing he did.

*****

The woman walked into her apartment wondering if Andros Poulos had gotten her mail yet. *What will he do?* She gazed at her corkboard full of photos. *I hope he takes that whore home,* she viciously thought. *Get her out of Pedro's life forever.*

"And then we can be together," she mumbled to the photo. "You and me and the baby." Sliding her hand over her stomach, she marvelled at the bump. She couldn't wait for them to have their baby, it would be such a gorgeous child with her papa's looks and her mama's smarts.

She checked the time. She'd been banned from the club after that fiasco the other week and had simmered for days, but it didn't stop her from standing outside the staff entrance every night waiting for him. To see him, to hear him, to smell him. God, he was beautiful.

Following him home every morning, she then followed that whore to school, coming back here to while away the days as he slept. *Maybe I should stay one day and be with him while she's not there? Yes…*a plan formulated. *Yes…that's what I'll do. I'll follow him upstairs and be with him while he sleeps.*

*****

Andros called his manager into the office. "Markos, you need to take over. I have business to attend to and will be gone for a few weeks." He collected some things from his desk.

"And where will you be in case you are needed?"

"I will call once I'm there. In the meantime…" He grabbed his briefcase. "Tell no one I'm gone. Regardless of *who* it is." He walked toward the door but stopped. "Especially…*him…*"

Markos nodded. "Yes, sir."

*****

Angelina woke Pedro when she got home, stripping off and massaging him until he rose to the occasion. She bounced up and down on him until she was a frenzied wild child, high on a natural drug.

He lay back and let her do her thing, watching as she threw her hair around, grabbed her breasts, screamed the place down, and let all the neighbours know she wanted him to fuck her.

"Ah," she gasped, her body weaving around. She pushed her hair back and flung it over one shoulder. "Oh, I've waited all day for that. To bounce up and down on your disco stick." She grinned and waited for his reaction.

Pedro cocked a brow *and* a lip. His arms were under his head and he was enjoying the start to his night. "Disco stick? Is that what we're calling it today?"

It always went down this way.

He'd come home from work and she'd be going to school. She'd come home from school all horny and wake him up for sex until he went to work and give his dick a new name.

She collapsed on top of him. "Yep. Oh, God, oh, God, oh, God you're so good." Her lips kissed his flesh and landed on his left nipple. "Oh, God, you're so good. How am I ever going to share you?"

His brow furrowed. "What do you mean, *share me?*"

She looked up and rested her chin on his chest. "How am I going to share you with all of the porn chicks you'll be fucking when you make your movie?"

He pushed her off and sat on the side of the bed.

"Hey," she protested. "I wasn't done."

"Then don't bring up pornos."

She spun around so she was sitting on his lap facing him. "What would be so wrong with doing that? It's huge right now."

"It's sex for money and movies." Pedro dropped

her on the bed and got up to stand by the window. "It's disgusting. I don't want to do it."

"You do it every day with me."

"That's different." He glanced back at her. "I love you, we're together, we have sex, together, with no one else. I don't pay you for it."

Angelina stretched languidly on the bed. "Have you *seen* a porno?"

"What?"

"Have you *seen* a porno?"

He turned. "No, I haven't."

"Then how do you know how disgusting it is if you've never seen one." She spread her legs.

"I…" He became distracted by the beautiful goddess that was so willingly open in front of him.

"Maybe you should watch a few, or go and see your brother's when it's out and *then* make up your mind."

He sighed, relented, and climbed between her legs. "Maybe I should."

October 1977

A week later, behind dark glasses, a cap, and clothes, Pedro rocked up to a movie theatre to see his brother's debut. Because Angelina wanted to see it, it had to be a weekend screening. And because Mike and Leon wanted to see it, it had to be a day screening, so Saturday it was, and Angelina brought Maggie for support.

They bought their tickets, entered, and sat up the back. Leon and Mike to Pedro's left, the girls to his right.

The theatre filled quickly with men and women. The lights dimmed, a few people cheered, and the movie started.

For Pedro, it was like every day on Mykonos. Carlos worked as a bartender by morning, spray tanner by afternoon, but by night, the masseur came out in him.

And so did his cock.

All ten glorious inches of it emerged onto the screen

for all to see, to the delight of everyone, bar Pedro, in the room.

"Whoo," Leon squealed. "Oh, my God, I want that in my mouth." He clapped excitedly.

Pedro just stared, embarrassed by his brother, yet turned on at the scenario.

The sex was fast and hot and all mouths, cock and pussy.

"Oh, my God, do that to me, do that to me." Leon fanned himself.

It faded to black after fifteen minutes, and Pedro let out a gush of air. "Oh, my God." He looked at the boys. Leon was faint in his seat and fanning himself, and Mike was wide-eyed, still staring at the screen.

He glanced at the girls. Maggie was red with embarrassment, her eyes to the floor, and Angelina had her hand between her legs under her skirt. "Hey." He pushed her hand away. "That's my brother."

"And he's fucking hot," she stated. "You didn't tell me your brother was *so fucking hot* because that publicity shot *does not* do him justice."

"You didn't ask." He stood and made his way out of the theatre. The others followed.

"You have to do something like that," Angelina said, taking hold of his hand.

He shook his head. "No, no I don't."

"Oh, my God," Leon sang, coming up to his side. "If your brother can do that imagine what *that* could do." He waved a finger up and down Pedro's body. "We know what you have under there." He glanced at Angelina. "Miss Thing knows what you got in your pants, and *we* know you've got everything else. You need to show it off." He wiped his forehead. "*Who knew* you brother was so goddamn fucking hot. I need to get me some of that."

"Carlos doesn't swing that way and neither do I," Pedro said, removing his hand from Angelina's and taking off down the street. They chased after him with Maggie and Mike trailing behind, chatting about things.

"Sweetie," Angelina cooed, catching up. "Considering what you look like and what you can do with your cock and the fact it's bigger than your brother's..." Pedro went red, and Leon's eyes were the size of saucers, "this is something you could make a lot of money doing."

"It's *not about the money*," Pedro said. "I make a thousand a night, it's not the money."

"Then what is it?" Leon asked. "You get nearly naked every night too; you clearly have no problem doing that."

Pedro thought about that. *He* DJed in shorts in a club full of women and men. *His brother* was now baring his Greek cock in movies. Why couldn't he? They made their way to a pizzeria where he slumped into a booth. "I dunno. Pornos?"

"Why not?"

He sighed. "I can't really think of a why not."

*****

"If my brother can do it, so can I," Pedro told Greta over the phone Monday morning. "When do I start?"

"How about today?" She tried to contain her excitement. "You can come into the office, we can talk about the movie we have lined up, you tell us what you think and show us the merchandise."

That made him feel uneasy, but he had made the decision. "I haven't had much sleep, but I can make it. Where do I go?"

Thirty minutes later he was standing in a luxurious office atop the Chrysler Building on the east side of Manhattan. The studio took up the whole floor, and he was ushered into the office of Greta Von Burro where Thomas, Carson and Stephanie stood around eagerly waiting for him.

"Pedro, do come in," Greta said. "Welcome, welcome. Come in."

He moved into the room and dropped his bag by the door. "I'm still not convinced this is a good thing," he said. "I'm not exactly comfortable with this."

"Oh, but we have the perfect movie for you." Stephanie moved closer to him. "It's perfect." Her eyes greedily moved up and down. "It's about a DJ who does private parties for the elite and ends up giving them so much more. If you know what I mean." She seductively licked her lips.

Now, Pedro was interested. "That's what I wanted to talk about."

"We'll have time for talking later," Greta said, moving to his side. "But right now we need to see if you've got what we want." Her hand wandered over his.

"No." Pedro stopped her hand. "*We talk now,* and I get it in writing before you see anything. I want a say in how this goes. If I'm gonna drop my pants and have sex with women I don't know, then I'm getting what I want in writing."

Greta saw the determination in his eyes. "And what do you want?"

"I want *this* movie, and any others I do, to be classy, tasteful and completely different to what my brother does. I want *that* in writing. *Before,*" he stressed the word, "I drop my pants."

Greta's eyes roamed up and down. "Martha, come and take a note."

Within the hour Pedro was signing a contract in duplicate.

"Well, now, we'll set everything up for this Saturday. I'm sure Eddie won't have a problem with you working for us once a week," Greta said, handling the contract.

"He did say we could have whatever we wanted," Thomas added, his eyes hungrily moving up and down the hunk of man meat before him.

"Now." Greta stepped back with the others. "Let's see the merchandise."

Pedro sighed inwardly, still unsure about everything that was happening, and pulled his shirt over his head. He let it fall to the floor and gave them a few moments to marvel at his tight abs and smooth tanned skin. His fingers went to his pants, unsnapped the button and slowly pulled down the zip, oh so casually pushing his pants down to his ankles. He stood and heard a noise behind him and saw staff with their hands and faces against the window of Greta's office peering at him. He slid his briefs down to join his pants and received cheers from everyone outside, and wide-eyed looks and even wider mouths from the four before him.

He flashed a cocky grin and put his hands on his hips. "So...think I can outdo my brother?"

*****

The woman had followed Pedro from Angelina's apartment to a midtown building and waited for him there. It was a long wait. A wait that was interrupted by people coming and going, even a security guard. She'd told him she was pregnant and did not feel well, asked if she could just sit and rest. He'd brought her a cup of water and some crackers. But after the first hour, she knew she needed to leave.

I'll have to go somewhere else, she thought, finally leaving when the guard asked if she wanted him to call an ambulance. "No, thank you," she said. "It's just my blood sugar. I feel better now." He nodded and helped her out the door. She took a moment to scan the area and decided to wait just down on the left; since the apartment was in that direction, she had a good chance of seeing him when he passed her. She waited just off an alley for another hour for him to come out. He walked by, and she followed as he went home. It was twelve o'clock, and she knew he wouldn't be leaving until six.

After watching him go inside, she went back to her own crappy apartment, not seeing the man in the car watching Angelina's place *and* her.

*****

Andros Poulos had flown by seaplane to Athens and a private jet to New York. He'd been there a few days, ensconced in a penthouse suite at the Waldorf-Astoria hotel, and had been keeping an eye on the comings and goings in Angelina's apartment. The man he'd hired, Stavros Christopoulos, had been watching the apartment, and Angelina and Pedro, twenty-four hours a day, seven days a week for the last few weeks since he'd known where they were. Now, he was in town and sitting in the car with Stavros.

"Who's that woman? The one with the red hair?" Andros asked.

"Dunno," Stavros said. "But I see her a lot. Follows Pedro around. I don't think he knows she does it."

"And what hours does he work?"

"Comes home about six-thirty in the morning and leaves about six at night."

"And Angelina?"

"Leaves about seven-thirty and comes home about three-thirty."

"Is she in all night?"

"Most nights."

"And when she's not?"

"At the club."

"Yes," Andros stroked his chin. "What is this club?"

"*Studio 69.*"

"Is it good?"

"The place to be. All the celebrities go there."

"Mmm, looks like I must go and see for myself. But

not before I deal with Angelina."

"When will that be?"

"Tonight, once he's gone and it's dark."

*****

Angelina came home at three-thirty and bounced away on top of Pedro as per their afternoon interlude.

"Ugh, what time is it?" he groaned.

"Three-thirty-five," she grunted.

"Ugh, Angie, I've only had three hours sleep. I need more." He lay there, and his eyes drifted closed.

"And how come you didn't get any sleep?" She threw her head back.

"Because I called up that producer and went to see her about doing the porno."

Angelina slowed to a stop. "You went to see her about doing the movie? Are you going to do it?"

He sighed. "Considering my position right now, it's not like sex with a stranger will be any different."

"But did you sign up to do it?" She grabbed his nipple and twisted. "Tell me."

"Oooh, you little." He shoved her hand away and bucked up underneath her. "Stop damaging the merchandise."

Laughing, she said, "Is that what they're calling it? I'm calling it the heat seeking missile today." Her hands flung her hair back. "What happened when they saw this delicious merchandise for the first time?" She clenched around him making him groan.

"Oh, honey, they loved it. The *whole staff* loved my

heat-seeking missile."

She clenched, he thrust.

"When do you do your first movie?"

He thrust, she clenched.

"This Saturday on Long Island."

"Ugh." She convulsed and subsided. "Can I come?"

"I think you just did."

*****

Andros watched Pedro head off to work at six-thirty and waited another two hours until it was dark. He exited the car, walked quickly across the street and entered the building. He knew which apartment was hers. He owned it, so, of course, he had a key. Making sure no one was watching, he slipped the key into the lock and slid inside. The TV was on, but silent, the radio was blaring, and he found Angelina dancing around naked in the bathroom, pinning her hair up.

"Daddy!" she exclaimed and grabbed a bathrobe from behind the door. "What are you doing here? How did you get in?"

Andros peered at the rumpled sheets. "This is what your life is?" He gripped her arms and ripped open her robe, yanking it from her body.

"Daddy!"

He pushed her down onto the bed and climbed on top of her. "This is what you've made of yourself?" he spat, staring into horrified eyes that looked like his own. "This is what you've become? A whore whoring out her body to the first man who'll have her?" He put his arm across her throat to hold her down. "This is what you want to be? A whore fucking any man who'll come between the legs you spread."

"Daddy," she pleaded through her tears as she grabbed at his arm. "Daddy, don't."

"Don't what?" he spat. "Don't call you a whore? Don't say you fuck men? Don't say you give your body to them?" He glanced down the length of her five-five frame and saw the smooth body of an eighteen-year-old girl. He hardened and grabbed her breast, crushing it beneath his hand, squeezing into his palm.

"Daddy, stop it." Angelina frantically tried to push his hand away. "You're hurting me."

"Does *he* hurt you?" Andros asked, shoving his hand between her legs. "Does he hurt you when he does this?"

"Ow, stop it. You're my father, you shouldn't be doing this, you can't do this."

"Well, see, that's where you're wrong, little girl." He shoved his fingers in and out of her womanhood as she screamed. "Your mother was a whore too, just like you. Or should I say, you're just like her, putting it out to any man that will take it. And wouldn't you know, she ended up pregnant. I never did find out if you were really mine…" He crushed his mouth to hers.

*****

The woman had followed Pedro to the club, but since she was banned, had decided to go back to Angelina's. Walking along in the dark, she'd seen a man leave a parked car and go into the building. Under the faint light of the street lamp, she thought she recognised him as Andros Poulos.

"He's here," she whispered excitedly. "He's here. Now he'll tell that whore not to mess with my man." She moved slowly and quietly along the street until she was across the road from the building; looking up, she saw two figures fighting in the bedroom. She knew it was the bedroom because she'd seen Pedro stand there naked and had managed to lie her way into their place one night when neither of them was home. The curtains were drawn, but the flimsy fabric still let shadows through.

Shadows that fought.

Shadows that had one another by the throat.

Shadows that picked up objects.

The smaller shadow picked something up and smashed it over the larger shadow's head.

The light went out.

Stavros was still in the car waiting for his boss. He hadn't taken any notice of the window, but had spied the woman who had followed Pedro earlier, standing down the road opposite the apartment looking up at it. He glanced up and saw the light was out. He sighed. That meant nothing. He went back to watching the woman who stood staring up. "What is she up to?" he muttered.

*****

Angelina stood over the body of her father. He wasn't

dead, but she had knocked him out with the lamp. He lay on the floor, and she stood there panting. She was battered and bruised and sore. But she hadn't been raised a Poulos for nothing; using her karate skills on her father didn't faze her.

Taking a deep breath she got to work. Throwing on a dress over underwear, she packed a huge overnight bag with clothes and toiletries, and packed her backpack with school books. She packed Pedro's belongings into his case and quietly left the apartment. She'd have to wheel the stuff down the road and try and flag a taxi. They couldn't go back there, and she'd made sure to grab their passports, her violin, and Pedro's money stash, leaving nothing valuable behind.

After making her way out the front door, she walked down the side alley to the next road over where she hailed a taxi. "Gramercy," she told the driver. She'd try and get a bed at Maggie's and leave their stuff there. But she had to get to the club and warn Pedro, because if he went home and her father was there, he'd be dead.

*****

Now, where's she going? the woman thought, spying Angelina sneak out and down the alley. She followed, watching her struggle with bags and a case. *That looks like Pedro's case. Why would she be sneaking out after dark with that?* She watched as Angelina made it down the alley and hailed a taxi. She hailed her own. "Follow that cab."

*****

Stavros looked up to see the woman wander across the road and down the alley beside the building. *'Bout time she left.* He checked his watch. Nine-thirty. *Boss didn't say how long to give them.* He glanced up and saw the light still out. *Must have moved into another room,* he pondered. *I'll wait until he comes out.*

*****

Angelina knocked on Maggie's door, but her mother answered instead. "Oh, hello Angelina, Maggie's not here…oh, my God, what happened to you?" She saw the luggage. "Did that boy of yours beat you up? Come in, come in." She grabbed the case and helped her inside. "Andrew, call the police."

"No, no, please no," Angelina begged. "It wasn't Pedro, believe me, he's working. I just, we, need a place to stay for the night. We'll find our own place tomorrow, but I didn't know where else to go. Please," she begged. "It wasn't Pedro. We just need a place to stay."

Andrew Boltworth came charging down the hall and saw the bite marks, scratches, blood and bruises on his daughter's friend. "If it wasn't your boyfriend then who was it?"

Angelina looked at both of them. "My father."

*****

The woman told the driver to stop outside of the

brownstone and made a note. "We can go now." She gave her address and sat back.

*****

Stavros saw the blue and red flashing lights coming down the road and wondered where they were going. Glancing up at the apartment he saw it was still dark. He watched the police car stop outside of the building, and two officers get out and go inside. *What the hell,* he thought, hoping Andros would come out soon.

The two officers, Devron and Burns, entered the building after getting a call about a domestic.

Devron looked at his notebook. "Third floor, apartment E." They climbed the stairs, found E, banged on the door and called out. "Hello, is anyone in there?"

The door to apartment F opened. "Oh, good," a short, middle-aged woman with a tight bun and stern face said. "You're here. Now tell them they need to stop fighting, or get out of the building."

"Ma'am," Burns said. "Do you know their names?"

"No, I don't, but she's out all day, and he's out all night. Get home at all hours, and when she gets home at three-thirty, there's screaming and groaning."

Burns and Devron exchanged amused glances.

"And do you know how old they are?" Burns asked.

"Young, teenagers, maybe, early twenties. Way too young to be living together out of wedlock. So please do something," she said and slammed the door.

Devron snorted. "A young couple working two different shifts and she wonders what the screaming and groaning's about."

Burns grinned and knocked again. "Hello, anyone home?" There was a sound. "What was that? Hello, can you hear me?" Another groan. "Sounds like someone's in trouble." Burns tried the handle and found the door unlocked. His hand slid in to flick the light on, and they held their pistols up. "Hello," he called, pushing the door open. "NYPD, I'm coming in."

They walked into the entrance and turned right into the lounge. There was nothing out of place, but as they moved into the back hallway, they saw the body on the floor.

Andros had come to and managed to crawl as far as the bedroom doorway.

"Sir, sir, are you all right?" Burns checked his pulse. "Thready, call for the paramedics."

Devron got on the radio while Burns turned on the bedroom light. The place was a mess. The bed was out of place, clothes were falling from hangers in the wardrobe, drawers were open and half empty. The bedside lamp was smashed on the floor, and there was blood on the white sheets.

"Sir, sir, who did this?" Burns bent down. "Can you tell me who did this?" He leant in closer.

"My daughter," Andros whispered. "Where is my daughter?"

"Bloody hell, there's a daughter," Burns said, helping Andros to sit against the wall. "Can you tell me what happened?"

"My daughter, where is my daughter?" Andros rasped.

"Was your daughter with you? Does she live here?"

"Yes, she was here. He did this. Where is my daughter?"

"Who's he, sir? The intruder?"

"No, no," Andros gasped through his busted ribs. "Her boyfriend."

"And what's his name?"

Andros licked his lips in concealed delight. "Pedro Stephanopoulos."

*****

Angelina left her things at the Boltworths' and took a cab to 69 where she managed to get in the back door because Pedro had introduced her to the guards when she'd gone with him. She managed to get Leon to tell him she was waiting backstage and now waited for him to take a break.

Half an hour later, he took his break and came rushing over to her. "Leon said you'd been in a fight. Oh, my God, what's wrong?" He gently held her face in his hands. "Oh, my God, look at you. What happened? Who did this? Are you hurt? Were you raped? Angie, what happened?"

"My father," was all she said.

*****

"Are you sure it was him who attacked you?" Burns asked.

"Yes," Andros said with steely determination. "He attacked me for seeing my daughter and then attacked her."

"And where would he be now?"

"At the club. *Studio 69.*"

"And what does he do there?"

"He's the DJ."

"And how long ago did this happen?"

"A couple of hours."

*****

Pedro was disbelieving. "Your father? He's here? He did this?" He shook his head and set off for the door. "I'm going to kill him."

She lunged after him to stop him. "No, don't, that's what he wants you to do. He'd want you to lash out at him so he can have you for assault."

He stared at her. "But he deserves—"

"I know," she soothed him. "But there's more."

Eddie walked backstage. "I heard there was a problem." He saw Angelina's battered face. "There's clearly a problem."

"Yes," Angelina said. "My father, Andros Poulos, is going to make trouble for Pedro. So you'd better make sure that there are witnesses to him being here all night because my father's on the rampage. If he's even my father." Her face dropped.

"What do you mean?" Pedro gently touched her arm.

"He told me while he was assaulting me that he may not even be my father. That's what gave him the right to try and…" She sobbed.

Pedro frowned. "What did he do to you?" The sick feeling in the pit of his stomach made him want to vomit.

"He sexually assaulted me and tried to rape me." She gulped and gasped trying to keep her emotions in check.

"I'm going to kill him," Pedro roared.

"No, no, no," Eddie said, putting a restraining hand on Pedro's arm. "You're going to do no such thing. Because *this* is what we're going to do."

*****

Stavros waited in the car, watching as an ambulance arrived and the attendants went upstairs. Ten minutes later he saw Andros being carted down on the stretcher.

"Fuck!" He banged the steering wheel. "How long has he been there and I've sat here waiting instead of going up. Fuck, fuck, fuck!"

He watched Andros being loaded into the van and started the car when the paramedics shut the doors and climbed in, waiting until they drove off before following.

*****

Pedro was on stage when the cops came for him. He saw them, kept an eye on them, and watched Eddie walk over to them and escort them backstage where they would talk to Angelina.

"And this is Miss Poulos. I believe she needs to talk to you." Eddie stood off to the side.

"Miss Poulos, we're here to talk about what your boyfriend, Pedro Stephanopoulos, did to you and your father."

Angelina stood up and turned around. "Don't you mean what *my father did to me*?"

They stared at the bruises and marks on her face, arms and neck.

"What about this?" She took her dress off to reveal bite marks, bruises on her thighs and scratches. "Pedro left for work at six-thirty, my father came through my door at eight-thirty and did this to me. Eddie here can vouch for Pedro's whereabouts at eight-thirty as can the incredibly rich women and men who have been in front of the stage since the place opened. Pedro was nowhere near my father when he was in my apartment."

Burns and Devron looked at each other, unsure of what to do. "Are you saying that your father did this to you and not your boyfriend? We need to make that clear because your father wants to press charges."

"That's exactly what I'm saying, and you can add sexual assault and attempted rape to that list." She watched their expressions change. "Oh, yes, apparently, my daddy may not be my daddy after all, and he used that as an excuse to get back at my dead mother, who, apparently, was also a whore."

Devron and Burns stared at Angelina. The red marks, the bruises. The swollen cheek and lip.

"I want to press charges against Andros Poulos for breaking and entering, trespassing, physical assault, sexual assault and attempted rape." Angelina donned her dress.

The officers exchanged a glance, unsure of what to do. "Wait here a moment ma'am." They moved to one side, and Burns used his radio. "This is Officer Burns.

We're at *Studio 69* talking to Angelina Poulos, the daughter of Andros Poulos. Mr Poulos has made a claim against his daughter's boyfriend of assault. Problem is, the daughter is also badly beaten and is blaming the father. She wants him charged."

"And the boyfriend?"

"Left for work at six-thirty and the father turned up at eight-thirty says the daughter."

"Well, then we have a problem. Take the daughter's statement. We'll need her to come in and be photographed, so, just bring her in."

"Yes, sir." They turned back to Angelina. "Ma'am, we're going to need you to come to the station and make a statement. But we also need to talk to Mr Stephanopoulos."

"But he—" Angelina started.

Burns put his hand up. "Just to get his side of the story."

"I'll get him to take a break," Eddie said.

A few minutes later, Pedro was backstage and holding Angelina in his arms. "What's all this about," he demanded. "Have you arrested him?"

"Not yet," Devron said. He was a six foot tall black man still in the closet, and at thirty-six, wasn't ready to come out of it, although, with Pedro standing before him, it was hard not to. "We need to ask you a few questions."

"And waste everyone's time," Pedro said.

"Do you know Andros Poulos?" Burns asked.

"Yes."

"How?"

"I was a DJ in his club in Santorini in May, June and part of July."

"Is that how you met his daughter?"

"Yes."

"How did you part? On what terms when you came to New York?" Burns asked.

Pedro glanced down at Angelina, and she nodded. "He found out we had started dating and attacked me in the alley behind his club. He threatened to kill me." He felt a little vulnerable standing in tiny gold shorts and knee-high lace-up gold boots in front of two strapping cops with guns.

"Did you tell the cops?" Devron asked, his suspicions aroused. He exchanged a look with Burns.

"On Santorini?" Pedro scoffed. "The cops are crooked and in the pocket of all the rich business owners."

"What happened then?" Burns asked, making notes.

"I hit him over the head to make him stop," Angelina said, her head on Pedro's chest. "He had Pedro pinned against the wall."

"What then?"

"He fell to the ground and his bodyguard came running out, and I knocked him out too. We ran to my house and got my things, then took a seaplane to Mykonos for Pedro to get his stuff. We flew to Athens and boarded a plane for here. I started at Juilliard in September."

"Had you heard from your father between then and now?" Devron asked, taking his own notes.

"No," Angelina said. "Nothing until tonight."

"And you've been here since…when?" Devron asked Pedro, eyeing the six feet of smooth Greek muscle before him.

"I usually get here about quarter to seven."

"And everyone can vouch for you?"

"Yes."

The officers put their notebooks away. "Okay, we need you to make a statement at the station. Can you come with us now, Miss."

"I want someone to go with me," she said. "I can call Mrs Boltworth."

"We can wait until she gets here," Burns said. "If you feel more comfortable."

"Yes." Angelina blinked. "I will."

Pedro looked down at her. "I should come."

"No, you finish your set," she said. "Then go to the station tomorrow."

"Are you sure?" He held her face. "Are you sure? If you want me there…"

"I'll be fine with Mrs Boltworth. We're staying with them until we can get our own place."

Pedro nodded. "And that will be tomorrow. Better get a car too."

"We'll go shopping tomorrow." She kissed him. "Go back to work."

He kissed her back. "You sure?"

"I'm sure."

"I'll see you tomorrow." He left her in Eddie's capable hands and went back to work.

*****

Stavros walked into the hospital and found his way into Andros's room. "Boss." He leant on the bed rail. "Boss."

Andros opened his eyes and saw him. "Where the hell were you when I needed you?"

Stavros went red. "I am embarrassed to say I thought everything was all right and you didn't need help."

"I didn't think I would," Andros said. "But my daughter has learned her skills and knows how to fight. At least I have put the blame where it belongs."

"And where's that?" Stavros asked.

"On Pedro Stephanopoulos."

"And how did you manage that?"

"By telling the officers that he beat my daughter and me."

"And what if she says he didn't?"

Andros closed his eyes. "Then I will have to find another way."

*****

Tuesday morning after work, Pedro went to the police station to give a formal statement about his knowledge of Andros Poulos and his whereabouts Monday night at eight-thirty. After two hours, he took a cab to the Boltworths' and found Angelina asleep in the spare room.

"I won't let you stay here with her; you'll have to find somewhere else to stay," Mrs Boltworth said as they stood in the doorway.

"That's fine," Pedro replied. "I'll go and get us an

apartment and a car, and we'll be out of your hair by tonight."

"That's not what I meant," she said.

"But that's our plan," Pedro told her. He kissed Angelina on the cheek and left to look at apartments.

*****

The police walked into Andros Poulos's hospital room at twelve-thirty.

"Ah, here you are," Andros said. "Have you caught the son of a bitch yet?" He waited while the officers traded looks.

"We've spoken to Mr Stephanopoulos, sir, and we won't be pressing charges against him."

"What?" Andros demanded with what little energy he had. "He did this to me. He assaulted my daughter and me. Where is Angelina? Have you found her? I want to see her."

The officers traded another look.

"We have found your daughter, Mr Poulos," Devron said. Andros quietened. "And she was at the club with Mr Stephanopoulos. We had a chat."

"A chat?" Andros said. "She was at the club with our attacker, and all you had was a chat?"

"We did more than that, sir." Burns' anger grew. He was a thirty year veteran of the force and had seen and heard a lot, but what he'd heard out of Angelina's mouth was just plain sick. "We took your daughter's statement down at the station."

"Good, good," Andros muttered. "Now you can

arrest that boy she is with."

"And we took photos of every part of her body. The scratches, the bruises, the cuts and marks."

Andros winced. "What he did to my poor little girl."

"And what your poor little girl told us was quite sick, Mr Poulos."

"Yes, yes it is." Andros waved a hand. "Now go and arrest the bastard."

Burns exchanged an amused glance with Devron. "If you insist."

"Yes, yes, I insist."

"Mr Andros Poulos, we are arresting you on suspicion of breaking and entering, assault and battery, sexual assault and attempted rape. You have the right to remain silent, anything you say or do will be used against you in a court of law. You have the right to an attorney. If you cannot afford an attorney, one will be appointed to you. Do you understand these rights as they have been read to you?" He snapped one side of the cuffs on Andros and the other to the bed rail.

"But-but-but what is this?" Andros raged. "What are you arresting *me* for? *He* is the one who assaulted us. *He* is the one who beat me up and hurt my daughter." He thrashed his arm back and forth. "Take these off me, you bloody idiot. *I am not under arrest. Pedro Stephanopoulos is under arrest.*"

"*No*, Mr Poulos, *you* are," Burns gleefully told him. "Your daughter revealed everything. How you walked in on her, pushed her down on the bed, and then groped her and tried to rape her. You sick son of a bitch," he spat, pointing his solid forefinger into Andros's face. "You're damn lucky it was her fighting back that landed you in here because if I'd caught you, you'd be down in the morgue. You…" he thrust his finger, "are under arrest." The two of them turned and left.

"You cannot do this to me," Andros screamed. "You cannot do this."

*****

With help from Eddie and Greta, whom Eddie had called, Pedro was able to rent a nice furnished apartment with security within a couple of hours. He had a red Corvette an hour later, and some flowers and chocolates for Angelina before picking her up at the Boltworths'.

"We have a nice view of Central Park, we're not far from Juilliard or 69," he told her as he piled their cases and bags into the trunk. Angelina had gone back to the apartment with Mrs Boltworth to get the rest of their things. "It's furnished, it has security, you'll love it." He took her into his arms and kissed her.

She snuggled into his chest. "As long as we're together and safe, I'm happy." He helped her into the car, much to Mrs Boltworth's anger, and Maggie's disappointment, and drove to their new home with underground parking for the new ride. They took the lift up to the seventh floor where he unlocked the door, opened it a crack, and then swept her into his arms.

She laughed as he moved inside. "You're only

supposed to carry me over the threshold when we're married."

"Well..." Pedro grinned cheekily. "I hope one day we will be."

That stunned her, for they had never discussed anything serious, let alone marriage. She was busy at school, he at 69, and they were still too young to be legally attached.

He set her down in front of the expansive window. "Look at that view."

She shook the thought out of her mind. "Oh, wow." They looked over the greenery of Central Park. "It's beautiful."

"And ours to look at every day." He ran back to bring the luggage in and locked the door. "Come, come and have a look." After flying over to her and grabbing her hand, he led her into the bedroom. "We have views here too and a nice bathroom. It's only a one-bedder, but that will do for now, won't it?" He slid his arms around her tiny waist.

"Yeah, it will do nicely," she agreed.

*****

Andros spoke to an attorney. "*What do you mean* they're not pressing charges against Pedro? *He attacked me.*"

"Mr Poulos," Miles Frankmore said. "Your daughter has pressed charges against *you, you...*" He emphasised with a finger pointed at Andros's chest. "They are not charging Mr Stephanopoulos because he was at work, and *your daughter* has named *you* as her attacker." In all these years he'd never come across someone as narcissistically delusional as Andros Poulos.

"But that is absurd."

"But that is the law."

"Then the law is an ass."

"Then get another lawyer."

"Fine, I will. You're fired."

"Good. Good day, Mr Poulos. Here's some free advice. Your daughter has taken out a TRO against you. You have to stay away from her or you'll be arrested. Do you understand?"

Andros waved him away. "You are not my lawyer. I do not have to listen to you."

Miles sighed. "No, but then I have a feeling you won't listen to anyone."

When he left, Andros called Stavros. "Get over here, I have a plan." Twenty minutes later Andros was spelling out plan B. "Shoot him."

Stavros raised a brow. "You want me to shoot him?" He looked around. "Where, when, how?"

Andros rolled his eyes. "Must I tell you how to do *everything*? When he is alone. When no one else is around. Preferably at night and with a gun."

"You want me to just go up to him and shoot him, or do it in a drive by?"

"I don't care. I want him dead. Leave me now." He had to make arrangements for getting out of the hospital. He wanted to go back to his hotel, but had been told he was no longer welcome, so needed an apartment.

*****

There was no sex for Pedro and Angelina. She hadn't wanted to, and he insisted they didn't. She needed to heal, and he had no problem giving her time, so they slept holding each other.

She kept waking, which was no surprise, and he barely slept because he wasn't used to sleeping at night. So he stood guard for any little sound, any little bumps in the nights. And when she woke from frightful dreams he soothed her back to sleep.

*****

Wednesday morning he drove her to school; even though it wasn't far, he wanted to make sure she made it safe and sound into Maggie's waiting arms. And she had insisted on going back, not wanting to let the assault stop her from getting on with her life.

"I'll be here to pick you up at three-thirty," Pedro called out the car window.

"Okay, see you then." She waved and walked off with Maggie.

Pedro went home and slept until three, and was back to pick her up. They went home and ate, and caught an extra two hours sleep before he had to go to work.

"Don't leave me here," she cried out, clinging to his hand when he went to leave.

He stopped. "Babe? What's wrong?"

"I'm scared," she said, tucking a strand of hair

behind her ear. "I don't want to be alone."

"You have locks and bolts and security downstairs." Pedro took her into his arms. "You'll be safe."

"I'll only be safe with you," she pleaded. "Please don't leave. Don't leave me alone. I'll sleep at the club in one of the offices. At least I know I'll be safe there."

Pedro raised a brow. "I don't think *anyone* is safe there."

"Please let me come." Her eyes pleaded with him.

He relented. "Okay, get your stuff."

She got her things and they went downstairs. Driving to the club, they parked out back and went inside. While Pedro changed, Angelina went in search of Eddie to see if she could sleep in an office.

The night began, but Pedro couldn't quite get into it. With everything that was going on he just couldn't feel good about anything, even his music. He nodded at Sara and Bev, who were there every night, and saw Martine slither up next to them.

Bridie McBall joined the group. She was an up and coming disco singer and had the latest hit that Pedro would be playing later. Dan Slayer, guitarist with rock band Slay Me, was dancing with Wednesday May, the star of the new Star Blade movie, *Killer Revenge*. She was young, she was blonde, and she was hot. Way too young and hot for Dan Slayer who was hitting forty.

Pedro looked around and saw Michael Jackson, Andy Warhol, Bianca Jagger, Debbie Harry and Grace Jones. He still got impressed by the big stars that came to 69.

*****

Stavros meticulously cleaned his gun, taking it apart, using a cotton stick to get into the crevices, and then putting it all back together.

He spun on a silencer and shoved in a cartridge. All it would need was one bullet. One bullet to do the job. One bullet to end Pedro Stephanopoulos. He went out to his car and got on his way.

*****

The woman knew what time Pedro got off work in the morning, which was a good thing since she didn't know where he lived. She'd gone back to the brownstone, but they weren't here. She'd gone back to the whore's apartment, but no one was there either. So waiting at the club was the only way to find him.

She checked her watch. Five-thirty. One hour left. She set off around the block to waste some time.

*****

Stavros pulled his car up to the alley at the side of the club. He needed to know what the best vantage point was so he could take the best and fastest shot.

He cruised by and saw stragglers leaving, but there weren't a lot of people in the street. He looked at his watch. Five-thirty. He cruised around the block.

*****

Pedro finished Bridie's song and did a shout out. "That was Bridie McBall's number one hit, *Rock Me, Roll Me*. Give a big shout out for Bridie!" The crowd jumped and hollered, and Pedro waved her up to the stage. "That's the third time we've played your song tonight Bridie; everyone keeps requesting it. You wanna say something to the crowd?" He held the microphone out to her.

"Thank you all for buying it, loving it, and wanting to dance to it." Her million dollar smile lit up the room. "Thank you all." She waved and left the stage in her skin-tight strapless sequinned jumpsuit and stilettoes.

"Bridie McBall, ladies and gentlemen. And up next is Slay Me's latest hit, *You Do It To Me*, and give Dan Slayer, the guitarist, a big rousing cheer."

"Whoo."

*****

The woman did a circuit of the block and checked her watch. Five-fifty. She sighed. *I should have just stayed in bed an extra hour and then come down,* she thought. She looked toward the stage door then to the cars parked in the alley and out back. Should she hide behind one of them? *I need to take cover when he comes out. I don't want him seeing me.* She glanced at her watch. *May as well walk around the block again.*

*****

Stavros came to a stop outside the club. He had no idea

if Pedro would be walking home, if he had a home, or if he'd catch a lift with someone else or take a taxi.

He sighed, thinking. *I need another couple of nights to scope the joint out. But no, no, no, Andros wants it done now. 'Now, now, now!'* He had yelled. *'I want it done now.'*

Taking notice of the position of everything he looked at his watch. Five-fifty. Sighing, he drove around the block.

*****

Pedro played a medley of Jackson Five songs to end the night to the crowd's delight. He saw Michael shy away into a corner and waved. Michael waved back, and Pedro left a twelve inch running at six on the dot.

The club closed and everyone was slowly escorted out. It usually took about an hour, and staff wrapped things up until the last straggler was gone.

Bev ran over to him and planted her lips on his. "Oh, my God, I love you, Pedro, are you single?" Her arms were around his neck hanging on for dear life.

He disentangled himself and Sara helped. "No, no I'm not."

"Come on, Bev." Sara took hold of her. "You've had a bit too much to drink. Let's get you home."

"I love you, Pedro. I don't care that you're not single. I want to fuck you anyway." She held out her arms as Sara dragged her away.

Pedro laughed, waved goodbye, and went to change.

*****

The woman came back around and saw people leaving. She looked at her watch. Six-ten. *It takes about twenty minutes to do the block, so I might as well stay here.* She wound her way down the alley and hid near a red Corvette and a pile of trash cans.

*****

Stavros came to a stop down the street from 69 and checked his watch. Six-ten. He could do another lap of the block and wait for all of the celebs to get out of the way, but he didn't know what time exactly Pedro left. He idled in place and decided to wait another ten minutes.

*****

Pedro talked with the staff members as they came and went in the staff room. Mike and Leon were some of the last to leave, and Pedro said goodbye. He went in search of Angie and found her in Stew's office, dead to the world on the couch.

He woke her. "Angie, time to go. You've got school, and I've got sleep."

She stretched and yawned. "What time is it?"

He checked his watch. "Six twenty-two."

*****

Stavros checked his watch. Six twenty-two. He slowly moved down the street until the alley came into view and he had a good line for the staff door at the back. He parked and waited.

*****

The woman watched the staff leave. Some were in cars, others walking; one fag of a black man even asked if she was all right and she told him to fuck off and move on. She checked her watch. Six twenty-five.

*****

Pedro said goodbye to those he came across as he walked Angelina through the back of the club.

"Can we go and get some breakfast first? I'm starving." She checked her watch. Six twenty-eight. "I don't have to be at school until eight."

"Sure, what do you want?" Pedro opened the door for her.

"Pancakes with maple syrup, bacon, scrambled eggs, the lot."

"And where are you going to put it all?" He laughed as they walked for the red Corvette.

The woman realised they were headed her way and ducked behind the large trashcans near the front of the car, watching.

Stavros saw Angelina with Pedro. "Fuck!" he swore and jammed his foot on the accelerator by mistake. The car was in park so the engine gunned, but the car didn't move.

The woman looked toward the sound and saw a panic-faced man stick his arm out of the window and aim a gun at Pedro. "No," she screamed and moved to cut it off.

The bullet tore through her and into Angelina. They both screamed and fell to the ground.

"Angie," Pedro yelled, catching her as she fell.

Stavros gunned the car and took off, screeching down the block.

Eddie and a few remaining staff members come running out the back door to see Angelina bleeding in Pedro's arms and another woman lying in the alley only a few metres away.

"What the hell happened, kid?" Eddie yelled.

"I don't know," Pedro sobbed, holding his hand over Angelina's wound. "She just went down, and a car screeched down the road. Help her."

Towels were held to Angelina's arm, and she groaned. "Pedro."

"Angie baby, everything's going to be all right, you'll be fine, just hang in there."

Staff members attended to the other woman. "She's alive," Stew yelled, "but unconscious. Must have hit her head when she fell." He wrapped a towel over the bullet hole. "How's Angie?"

"Hanging in there," Pedro yelled back, holding her tighter. "Come on, Angie, come on, baby."

*****

Stavros belted down the road into screeching turns. He needed to get away so no one could tail him. "What a cock-up. Fuck, fuck, fuck, fuck, fuck!" He banged the steering wheel and headed back to his motel in Jersey. His boss was not going to like this.

*****

They loaded Angelina into the back of the ambulance and Pedro climbed in next to her holding her hand. "You're gonna be okay, baby, you're gonna be okay."

The paramedic took her blood pressure and said, "She's stable and hanging in there."

Pedro stroked her hair. "Yeah, she's hanging in there."

The woman was loaded into another ambulance. "My baby," she murmured, her hand going to her stomach. "Pedro's baby."

Stew overheard her and frowned. This woman was pregnant to Pedro? He didn't seem like the type to cheat on Angelina, but then who knew.

*****

Stavros made the call. "It didn't work."

"What do you mean it didn't work?" Andros said. "You were supposed to shoot him. How did it not work?"

"Because a woman got in the way and she was shot instead…plus…"

"Plus?"

"Angelina was there. The bullet hit the woman and

redirected into Angelina."

Silence…

"You shot my daughter?"

"The bullet ended up in her…I think…I didn't shoot her on purpose."

"You shot my daughter," Andros screamed down the line. "How dare you shoot my daughter!" He slammed the phone down. "What's the old saying, if you want the job done right you'll have to do it yourself."

Stavros felt the panic rise. It started boiling in his stomach and slowly crept up his insides to settle in his throat. It choked him, made him unable to breathe. *This is getting out of control,* he thought. *This is nuts, insane, psychopathic. After what he did to Angelina he screams at me for cocking up a shooting. No, he's standing on the edge, and someone has to take the fall.*

*****

Hours later, Pedro was pacing back and forth in the hospital when Eddie stepped out of the elevator with Greta Von Burro.

"Pedro, how is she?"

He stopped in a daze and turned. "Still in surgery. They said she should be okay because it's in her shoulder, but even then there's severe bleeding and nerve issues."

"This is a very good hospital," Greta told him. "The best doctors work here."

Pedro flashed a lost smile. "I know. I told them

money was no object. Whatever they needed to do, do it. Whatever specialists they needed, get them. They said they're taking care of her."

"That's good." Greta laid a hand on his arm. "She's in good hands."

"Yeah. What about the other woman?" Pedro asked.

"She's being looked at in emergency. Flesh wound, apparently, but knocked her head when she fell. Stew's with her to make sure she gets good care too," Eddie said.

*****

Stew was standing outside the cubicle as the woman was being examined, wondering about the words she'd muttered. "Oh, Doctor," he called to the woman who'd just left the cubicle. "How is she?"

The doctor took a clipboard from a nurse and signed her name. "Flesh wound that will be stitched up. Has a concussion from hitting her head. Some dizziness, fades in and out. We'll keep her in overnight for observation to make sure she's okay."

"Did you check on the baby?"

"Baby?" The doctor's head turned. "Did she say something about being pregnant?"

"She muttered, *the baby, the baby*, when she was put in the back of the ambulance," Stew said.

"Mmm, we'll have to check that out, thanks for telling me." She went back in to the cubicle.

Stew paced, sat, and paced some more over the next twenty minutes while machines came and went and the doctor finally emerged.

"Well, I can categorically say she is not pregnant," she said. "But…" She glanced at the cubicle. "She kept insisting she was. So I'm going to call a psyche consultant and make sure she's checked on through the night."

"Thank you, Doctor." Stew decided to stick around until she had been taken to the psyche ward.

*****

It was another half an hour before the doctor emerged from the operating theatre with news on Angelina.

"Doctor, how is she?" Pedro rushed to his feet.

"She'll recover. The bullet went into her left shoulder. She may not recover full use for a while, but with physiotherapy and time, she should."

"Can I see her?"

"She's being taken into recovery, you can see her once they take her to her room."

Pedro nodded. "Of course. Thank you, Doctor." They shook hands.

Officers Burns and Devron stepped out of the elevator.

"God, not you two," Pedro said. "What is it now? He found out about his daughter and wants to see her?"

"Actually, Mr Stephanopoulos, we heard about the shooting and came to get statements."

"Have you caught the guy who did it?" Pedro asked.

The officers exchanged a look. "Unfortunately no."

"You can start with her father," Pedro told them.

116

"Considering what he's done to her I wouldn't put it past him to try this."

"That's what we were wondering," Burns said. "We've been to the scene and had a good look. Considering your involvement with Mr Poulos, we're wondering if it wasn't *you* the shooter was trying to get."

Pedro frowned. "Me? Why would he…" He nodded when he realised. "Andros is trying to kill me, but got her by mistake because she's not normally there."

Burns nodded in agreement. "If he hates you that much we're thinking, unless you have other enemies, that he took a hit out on you to get you out of his daughter's life."

"Well…" Pedro grinned wryly. "He's the only enemy I have that I know of."

"Then we'll look into that," Burns said. "We'd like to talk to Miss Poulos. We can come back later today."

"Do that," Pedro said. "She's just gone to recovery and won't be out for a while."

Burns nodded again. "Right, now, Mr Monteif, we heard there was another victim. Was she a staff member?"

"No," Eddie said. "Just some woman in the alley. No one knows who she is, but one of our guys is downstairs with her now."

"We'll go and chat with them then, gentlemen, ma'am," Burns turned to go.

The elevator surged to a stop and Stew stepped out.

"Oh, wait," Eddie called to the officers. "Here he is now."

Stew walked over and eyed the cops. "Caught the son of a bitch yet?"

"Not yet, sir. But we'd like a word with the other victim."

"The nutjob?" Stew saw their expressions at his word. "She's just been taken to the psyche ward for observation."

"What's wrong with her?" Pedro asked.

"Mumbled something about a *'baby, Pedro's baby'* when she got carted away," Stew said, watching Pedro's expression.

"Wait." Pedro shook his head. "What do you mean *my* baby? I've only been with Angelina." He saw the curious stares the others gave him.

"That's the rub," Stew said. "The bullet only grazed her arm, and she hit her head when she fell, resulting in a concussion. I spoke to the doctor, told her she had mumbled something about a baby, and she went back in to check. Turns out, she's *not* actually pregnant. Hence the night in the psyche ward because she kept insisting she *was* pregnant." Everyone looked at him. "We've got a whack job on the loose."

"Where's the psyche ward?" Pedro asked.

"Fifth floor," Stew replied. "I've just come from there."

"And Angelina's going to be here on the second." Pedro sighed. "Good, keep her away from us." He turned to the officers. "And keep Andros Poulos away as well. I want an armed guard on Angie's door at all times. If this was an attempt on any of us then who's to say he won't try again."

The officers nodded. "We'll get one down here right away," Burns said, and they left to visit the psyche ward.

*****

Andros stalked around his apartment. "No one gets the better of me," he hissed. "*No one.* I have to do something to get rid of that Stephanopoulos kid, but what? What can I do…what can I do…?" He thought about it. Pedro worked in a club where rumours of drugs and alcohol were rich and rife. He'd dealt in drugs at his own club and knew how to set someone up for a downfall. *Now, where will I get drugs in New York?* He couldn't have them flown in; he'd have to get them from a supplier.

He made a few phone calls to the suppliers he did use and was given a name. Just out of New York on Long Island, was a very wealthy man who dealt in all manner of things who could easily get his hands on a few kilos of coke. He made a call and discussed business. "Good, good," Andros concluded. "I don't know when I'll need it for, but soon, very soon."

"All right, then why don't you come to my house on Saturday night? We are having a little party upstairs while a movie is being filmed outside in the backyard."

"What kind of movie?" Andros's curiosity was piqued. Maybe he could be in it.

"A porno."

*****

Pedro was by Angelina's side when she woke. "Hey, baby, sweetie, how do you feel?" He pushed her hair out of her eyes and off her forehead.

"Weak," she murmured drowsily. "Tired." She licked her lips and swallowed. "Thirsty."

He poured some water into a small cup and held it to her lips. "Here, just a sip."

She drank and lay back on the pillows with a sigh. Looking around the room she vaguely remembered what had happened. Her right hand went to her arm that was in a sling. "What happened? What was that?"

Pedro licked his lips and wondered where to start. "You were shot," he finally said.

Her eyes widened as she turned her head to look at him. "What? What do you mean, shot? By who? My father?"

Pedro gave a brief nod. "We think it might be your father. Who else would it be? But apparently, a guy in a car was waiting for us, and he fired a shot. It hit another woman in the arm and bounced off her into your shoulder." He paused. "The cops think it was me he was aiming for."

"You?" she said. "Why would…" The light dawned. "My father. Of course *he'd* want to kill you." She sighed. "But it got me instead. You said it hit another woman? How is she?"

"Ah, in the psyche ward under supervision." Pedro glanced around the room.

"Why did they put her in there if it's an arm wound?"

"Because she kept saying *'my baby, my baby'*, but she's not actually pregnant. So they're keeping her under observation for the concussion, in case it caused her memory loss, or memory failure, whatever it is."

"Oh, poor thing," Angelina said. "To lose a baby."

"She wasn't actually pregnant, so she didn't lose it."

"Either way, she must be devastated and in need of some mental help."

"Which is why they put her in the psyche ward," Pedro said.

"Well, if that's the best place for her," Angelina said. "Then I hope she gets the help she needs."

"Speaking of help." Pedro changed the subject. "There's an armed guard on your door all day every day until you get out. So hopefully your father won't be able to try anything."

"If he's after you, he won't come near me," she replied sleepily.

"Maybe, maybe not. The other thing is, Greta wants me to shoot a movie on Saturday night, but with everything that's happened, I'm not sure now."

"Do it," she urged, covering his hand with her good one.

"But I—"

"Do it," she repeated. "Don't let this stop you from fulfilling your contract. I'm a bit pissed that I won't get to be there and watch you in action, but I expect a copy for myself so I can watch it. And then we can re-enact it so I get to fulfil my fantasies of fucking a DJ at a party."

Pedro snorted. "I'd say you've already done that one. Just look at the way we met."

She laughed and clutched her arm. "Ow."

"Hey, take it easy." He put his hand out. "Take it easy."

"Do it," she said. "For me."

He gazed into her beautiful brown eyes and saw his forever. "Okay."

*****

Eddie gave him the rest of the week, which was only a few days, off, and he spent Thursday night through Saturday morning at the hospital. In the afternoon he drove out to Long Island to the impressive and indulgently wealthy estate of some rich person. He didn't know who, but he definitely wanted to meet the owner.

After parking next to the company van, he was escorted through the luxuriously excessive interior to the backyard. It was in the process of being set up to look like a private party. DJ booth on the right, a long cabana with flowing curtains that ran across the pool in front of him, and a bar with waiters on the left. It looked like a very expensive pool party indeed.

"Pedro, darling." Greta walked over to him and took his hand. "Come, let me run you through what's happening." She led him to the DJ booth. "You're going to be playing here." They stood overlooking the see-through dance floor that showed the pool's reflection underneath. "There will be lots of hot young women dancing, flirting, sexy, almost no clothes. You'll be here in tuxedo pants and open shirt. You'll give them the look, they'll flirt, there'll be lots of swirling curtains, it will be sexy, it will be hot, it will be fucking good."

Pedro grinned. "Do I get to say anything?"

"Oh, darling, all you need to do is stand there and look sexy."

He laughed. "Is that all!"

"Well…" Greta smiled wickedly. "And get naked and have sex. Let me show you to your dressing room."

*****

Andros took a limousine to Long Island. Stavros wasn't worthy of driving him anymore, so he'd hired a car for the night. They pulled up to the mansion and he gave it a critical once over. *I need to get myself one of these*, he thought. *Maybe I should move to New York and open a club. There are so many opportunities, it's a great city.*

He was escorted upstairs to the lounge area that spread the entire back part of the room and met Nedro Scarvo, an Italian French mix of passion and hatred; for himself and others.

"Andros Poulos," he said, putting out his arms in welcome. "Come, come, we will party, yes."

Andros made his way over to Nedro and accepted the drink the waiter offered. "This is quite a place you have here. I think I might like one of my own."

Nedro laughed loud and long. "Well, you can't have this one, but maybe I can help you there. Come, come, sit and let's enjoy the movie." He pointed to a couple of lounge chairs on the balcony.

"Has it started already?" Andros asked, seeing a

group of hot-looking women dancing under the cabana. Cameras were everywhere moving back and forth catching the women in the setting sun.

"Yes, yes. They told me it's a mostly silent movie, so they need more footage than anything."

"And you said it was a porno," Andros said. "I've never seen a porno being made before."

"Sit back and enjoy," Nedro said. "And drink, drink."

Andros raised his glass and kept his eyes on the nearly naked women.

*****

Pedro stood in his pants and shirt having a bit of make-up put on. "Do I need this?" he asked.

"Just to even out your tone and get rid of shine," the make-up woman replied.

"Pedro," Stephanie purred. "It's time to go on. Now, let me fill you in."

"Greta did that this afternoon."

"Well, let me tell you too. We'll tell you when to go on, and it doesn't matter if you make mistakes, just keep on going and we'll edit it out later." She led him to the door. They'd taken over the ground floor for the movie and were exiting through the huge dining room. "You casually walk over, get behind your booth, and start doing your thing. One of us will indicate to you when to pull your shirt out so it hangs, and at some stage we'll let you know when to get down and start dancing. From there you just do your thing."

"My thing," Pedro repeated. "Which is?"

"Being so fucking hot and sexy." Stephanie arched a seductive brow.

Pedro shook his head at the situation he'd gotten himself into.

"So," Stephanie went on. "We're just about ready." She checked Pedro's clothes and undid another button on his shirt, running her hands over his torso. A sigh escaped from between her lips. "Delicious."

"And not yours," Pedro reminded her.

"Ugh, I hate that," she muttered. "Okay, get ready to walk over and…go."

Pedro strolled over to the DJ booth, donned his headphones and got on with it. It was going to be a long night, but at least he'd have fun spinning the discs.

For the next three hours camera crews kept rolling, and somewhere between hours two and three girls disappeared, leaving just three for Pedro to do. He had pulled his shirt out of his pants two hours ago and was slick with sweat. He eyed the beautiful girls on the dance floor waving at him to come over.

In a blur of billowing curtains, he left the booth, danced over to the girls and ground against them. They danced, they gyrated, they removed their clothes in a slow sensual feast for the eyes. His shirt, their dresses, his pants. Their hands slowly pulled down his underpants and he stepped out of them. The gyrating, grinding and dancing continued. The curtains billowed, the cameras moved in, zooming in on the prize it was after.

One girl backed onto him and they kept on dancing. Just like the first time he'd fucked Angelina in the club. He held the girl by the hips as they moved and the other two slithered up and down on him, on each other. He kissed them, touched them, and fucked them one by one.

*****

"Who is that man?" Andros asked from the balcony. "And where did he come from?"

"He's the DJ in the movie," Nedro said. "Some Greek kid called Stephanopoulos."

The realisation hit Andros square in the eye. "*Pedro* Stephanopoulos?"

"Yeah, that's it." Nedro called to the waiter. "Another drink."

Andros boiled with fury. "Do you have that parcel I asked about?" If there was ever a more opportune time to get him back, it would be now.

"Yes. Do you want it now?"

"Yes."

"Okay." Nedro waved over his henchman and spoke in his ear. The man left and came back a few minutes later with a box. "Here," he told Andros.

Andros took the box and looked inside. It was a block of cocaine. "Excellent," he hissed. "I need your help." He told Nedro of his plan, and Nedro passed it on to his henchmen who took the box and left the room.

"Good, good." Andros sat back in his seat. "It will end tonight."

*****

The cameras stopped rolling and Pedro backed off. "You girls okay. I didn't hurt you or anything?"

The girls stared dazedly. Being fucked by an eleven inch cock was oh so mouth-wateringly good.

"Oh...I'm fine," the blonde murmured, her voice husky. "In fact, I could do that again."

"Me too."

"Me three."

"Pedro." Greta came over. "Excellent, excellent. We got some fantastic footage." She turned to the girls. "Get dressed and go home. Excellent job. Pedro darling, get your clothes back on, we're going to do a photo shoot with the city lights as the backdrop. Come."

He picked up his clothes and followed her down the back to an old stone fence. The city twinkled in the distance.

"Get dressed darling and we'll take some photos."

He quickly slid on his pants and shirt before the stylist came over and adjusted everything just artfully so. His shirt was open, collar up. He had make-up reapplied, and the lights lit up his blue eyes.

"Oh, that's perfect," Greta told the photographer. "Put your hands on your collar as if you're pulling it up," she called after a few shots. "That's it. Head down, smile, look hot, look sexy, look like you've just fucked the person looking at you."

The photographer laughed and kept on snapping.

"Look like you want to fuck every woman looking at you," Greta continued until the roll of film was done. "And we're done. Good job, everyone. Let's pack up and go home. Pedro," she called him over. "Awesome job.

Get changed and go see that girl of yours. I'll let you know when we do the next one."

"Thanks, Greta." Pedro went back to the house to change.

*****

Upstairs, Andros watched him flirt with the camera and that woman. He'd fucked three women and was probably going home to his Angelina. "Manwhore," he spat and watched Nedro's man come back.

"Is it done?" Nedro asked.

"It is done."

*****

Pedro changed his clothes, thanked the staff, and walked out to his Corvette. He gunned the engine, thrust the throttle, and spun out of the driveway to speed down the highway, wanting to make it back to Angie.

Changing gears, he hit the accelerator, feeling the grunt of the engine beneath him. As he neared the city, he changed speed and hit the brakes...

Nothing...

He hit the brakes...

Nothing...

"What the fuck!" He pumped the brake, shifted gears and slammed the pedal into the ground. "Why aren't you working?" he yelled, speeding across the Queensboro Bridge into the city. He swerved to avoid cars, pumping the brakes all the way. "Oh, my God."

He saw the end of the bridge. "Oh, my God." He slammed on the brake and spun the wheel.

*****

Andros left soon after Pedro. "I want to see what happened," he told Nedro. "To see if my plan worked."

Nedro slapped him on the back. "I hope it did, and you get that boy out of your life." He walked him to the door. "I hope it goes well."

"So do I," Andros muttered. "So do I."

*****

Pedro's eyes slowly blinked open. Bright twinkling lights flashed before him, voices floated around him, but they were dull, as though he was under water. He heard a siren and tried to move. "Ugh," he groaned. The pain shot through his head like a lightning bolt, making him see stars on top of the bright light.

"Ugh, what happened?" He tried to move his legs, but they didn't move far. He tried to move his arms and could move them enough to feel his head. "Ugh." He looked at his hands. They were slick with red fluid. "Oh, God."

"Don't try to move, we'll get you out," someone yelled and hands came through the smashed window. "Just sit still, we're going to check you out first."

He felt hands go around his neck, pull his eyes down, saw a light flash in them. He felt the rest of him being checked and heard more sirens. "Ugh." He tried to move.

"*Don't move.* We're going to get you out," the voice came again.

Somewhere in the back of his mind he heard machinery, metal on metal, and slowly, piece by piece, the people around him made headway.

A wide hard thing went around his neck, something sharp pierced his arm. He felt something else flow into his veins like a metallic flood oozing through him, *into* him. He groaned again, he moved again. He *was* moved and he was free.

Flat, lying on something cold and hard, he was wrapped and covered. The bright lights twinkled. The people's voices became clearer, yet distant. He groaned. He was moving, feeling sick, dizzy, suffocated by everything around him, on top of him.

"Well, well, well," someone said. "You just can't keep away from us can you, Mr Stephanopoulos. We'll see you at the hospital."

The driver of Andros's limousine saw the flashing lights and hit the brakes, slowing down on the bridge.

"Why are we stopping?" Andros demanded. He was pissed off because he hadn't seen any sign of Pedro or his smashed car on the way back from Long Island.

"Police and paramedics ahead. Could be an accident, sir."

Police? Accident?

Andros rolled down the window and peered out. Could it be? Oh, yes, could it be?

They slowly drove past the accident, and Andros

saw the Corvette smashed in half, bent around a pole, and poor little Pedro being put into an ambulance. He smiled. The cold, calculating smile he used for winning. "Oh, yes, little boy," he hissed. "I have won and you are done." He noticed the officers hanging around looked like the ones who'd come to the apartment that night, and then to see him in the hospital to arrest him. "Well, it's not me they'll be arresting for this," he muttered. "Goodbye forever, Pedro Stephanopoulos. You may not be dead, but I hope you go down for life." He rolled the window up and they drove away.

Ten minutes later Pedro was rolled into emergency at the same hospital as Angelina. The officers had directed them there so they would be together. He lay still as he was shunted back and forth from x-ray to emergency before being taken to a room. The brace was removed, the needle was taken out. He was given painkillers. His eyes closed against the stream of lights, faces and voices.

*****

The next morning, Andros read the paper hoping for something about Pedro. But there was nothing. "Guess it's too early for his demise," he said.

*****

Pedro's eyes opened to find Angelina beside his bed. "Hey," he croaked. "You should be resting." He reached out a hand to stroke her face.

"What happened?" she asked, fear, anger and sadness in her eyes. "What happened?"

A small smile slid across his lips. "I don't know. You tell me."

She frowned. "You don't remember?"

His frown replicated hers. "No."

"You crashed your car."

He blinked. He breathed. He blinked again. "What?"

"You crashed your car on the way back from Long Island."

He racked his brain, and slowly the pieces became clear and connected. "Oh," he groaned. "I'm starting to remember."

"Good. Then you can tell us what happened," Burns said from the doorway. He and Devron walked in.

"You guys are everywhere," Angelina said, adjusting her blanket. She was in a wheelchair and had been brought in earlier when she'd been told Pedro was a patient.

"Well, it seems that the two of you keep popping up on our radios," Devron replied. "We've been told that whatever happens, to stay on your cases."

"Speaking of the case, there was a block of coke in your trunk. Care to tell us where that came from?" Burns asked, tapping his pen on his notebook.

Pedro blinked dazedly. "Coke?"

"He doesn't do coke," Angelina scoffed. "*We* don't do coke or any other drugs."

"Then why did we find a block of it in the trunk of your car?" Devron stood with his hands on his hips.

"Did you also find I had no brakes?" Pedro asked, rubbing his face. "My brakes failed. No matter what I did, no matter how hard I pumped, the brakes wouldn't work. I think that's why I crashed. I couldn't stop."

The officers exchanged a glance. "Where were you yesterday, Mr Stephanopoulos? From the beginning."

"I was here at the hospital with Angie until twelve-thirty. Then I went to Long Island to shoot a movie. I was there until after midnight."

"Where on Long Island?"

"A huge mansion. 1212 Montauk Way. I don't know who owns it. My boss hired it for the movie."

Burns traded a glance with Devron. "We're just going to check on something," he said and stepped outside to radio headquarters. "This is Officer Burns, can you tell me who lives at 1212 Montauk Way on Long Island and if we've had any dealings with him?"

"You got a feeling?" Devron asked, leaning against the wall next to the door.

"Yep."

"1212 Montauk Way belongs to Nedro Scarvo. We have no personal dealings with him, but Long Island police have. Known drug kingpin and deals in anything else you want."

"Thanks." Burns clicked off.

"Well?" Devron asked.

"I've got a bad feeling," Burns said, and they re-entered the room. "Did you happen to meet a man by the name of Nedro Scarvo yesterday at all?"

Pedro thought. "No."

"Why don't you tell us what did happen."

Pedro swallowed. "I got there, was led through what would happen in the movie. Went over it with the producer and director. Ate, worked out, watched them set up, film, talked to the girls in the movie, got dressed, had make-up. Went on stage and filmed until well after dark. Then did a photo shoot, went in, changed and left."

"About what time?"

Pedro thought some more. "I looked at my watch at…ten past twelve when I was getting dressed. So, a few minutes after that."

"And you never met Scarvo?"

Pedro slowly shook his head. "No. I didn't meet anyone outside of the movie. I didn't meet an owner. No one. Why?"

Burns finished taking notes. "Because Scarvo is Long Island's biggest drug dealer yet no one can get him on anything. Now you say you'd never been there before and your boss hired the place."

"That's right."

"Where was your car?"

"Out front next to the company's production van."

"And you didn't go out to it at any time?"

"No."

"Did anyone else that you know of?"

"No. That's not to say no one did, but I didn't see and don't know if anyone did."

Burns sighed. Considering the kid had been at a drug dealer's to shoot a movie that wasn't organised by him, that meant someone else wanted to set the kid up. "You said your brakes failed."

"Yes." Pedro nodded. "I just couldn't slow down no matter how hard I pumped. In fact, it felt empty, light, as if there was nothing there and the pedal just moved up and down."

Burns frowned. He'd heard that before. "You rest, and we'll go and see what the tech boys have found with your car. We'll be in touch."

"What the hell is going on?" Angelina said from her chair when they'd left. "First a shooting, and now drugs and a car crash. Was there anything wrong with your brakes before?"

"No. And why should there be? It's a brand-new car."

*****

The woman was in her apartment. She'd been let out a few days earlier from the psyche ward. What the hell was she doing in there? She ran through the events. Waiting for Pedro, seeing him with that whore, hearing the car, seeing the gun pointed, jumping in front of Pedro, searing pain in her arm and then nothing.

She looked at her right arm. The stitches would need removing and the bandage changed, but other than that she and the baby were okay. Her baby. The baby they'd told her she wasn't having. She'd accused them of lying. They put her in the psyche ward believing the concussion had knocked a screw loose. Well, not only had it *not* knocked a screw loose, but it had made her more determined than ever to deal with Angelina and have Pedro once and for all.

After all, their baby couldn't come into the world with just one parent. She had to put her plan into action as soon as possible. *And no one,* she thought as she remembered the man's face from the shooting, *will get in my way.*

*****

Burns and Devron walked into the building the force used to pull cars apart. They saw the wreckage of the Corvette and Devron whistled. "That must have been some car."

"Yeah, and some crash," Burns replied. The wreckage was laid out, and it was now a mere shell of what it once was.

"Gentlemen, Investigator Grosner. You are here about the Corvette, yes?" the five foot five man in the grey overalls asked. At fifty-five he was balding rapidly and just had a ring of brown hair around his bald spot.

"Yeah." Devron nudged a piece on the tarp. "You find anything?"

"Like a cut brake line, you mean?"

Burns and Devron's heads swivelled to the man. "His brakes were cut?"

"Yep, nothing else. The car is only what, a few weeks or months old. Everything is in pristine condition except for the brake line." He signed off on some paperwork. "I'll get my report typed up and over to you in the next day or two. Anything else?"

Burns shook his head. "No. Thanks for that, can't wait to read it." He and Devron left. "Well, what do you know? *Another* attempt on the life of Pedro Stephanopoulos. What is with that kid that makes Andros Poulos hate him so much?"

"We don't know it *was* Poulos. He was at Scarvo's house for twelve hours," Devron reminded him.

"True." Burns got into their car. "But what reason does Scarvo have for hating him? As far as we know, he's never met Scarvo, but we *do* know Poulos does drugs back in Greece. Both Pedro and Angelina confirmed that."

"Well," Devron said. "Whoever it is, he's a sick son of a bitch and probably won't stop until the kid is dead."

Burns revved the engine. "So, *we'll* just have to stop him."

*****

Greta, Stephanie, Thomas and Carson piled into Pedro's room.

"There you are, darling. We heard all about the accident from Eddie and came to see how damaged you were." Greta laid a bunch of flowers on the table. "How are you?" She glanced at Angelina. "And who's this unlucky girl with the sling?"

"His girlfriend." Angelina raised a brow. "You must be Greta Von Burro, the woman that got him into this mess by hiring a drug dealer's house to film your movie."

Greta arched a brow as Stephanie, Thomas and Carson took a step back. "Drug dealer? Nedro Scarvo?

Huh, that's hilarious."

"So is the block of cocaine the cops found in Pedro's trunk after the accident," Angelina spat icily.

The others gasped in horror. "A block of coke, oh, no, that had nothing to do with us," Greta rushed to say. "If there was anything going on there we have no idea what it was. We just hire homes for the location. We don't care what the owners do or are."

"And there's the problem," Angelina said. "His car was sitting in a drug dealer's driveway all day and night, and when he leaves there's a block of coke in it and the brakes have been tampered with. Clearly, someone wanted him dead or caught and arrested."

"Whoa, whoa, what?" Greta put her hands up in protest. "Back up a minute. Your brakes were tampered with?"

"We think so." Pedro nodded. "They gave way; I didn't have anything to stop with."

"Jesus." Thomas crossed his chest. "Who'd want a gorgeous specimen like you dead?"

"My father," Angelina said simply. "He probably had Nedro set him up."

"Who's your father?" Greta asked.

"Andros Poulos."

"What does he look like?"

"Five ten, black hair, tan, wears suits all the time. Trim, but well built."

Greta recalled last night when she'd left for her own car and watched a man climb into a limousine not long after Pedro had left. "There was a man fitting that description who left just a few minutes after you," she told Pedro. "I'm sure of it."

Angelina sighed. "Of course it would be. If my father wanted drugs, then he'd find a supplier in New York, and who supplies…Nedro Scarvo."

"Apparently, he cuts brake lines too." Burns stood in the doorway with Devron, having been eavesdropping on the conversation. "Our guy says your brakes were cut. Everything else about the car was fine. Brand new." They walked into the room. "Someone's out to get you, Mr Stephanopoulos."

"My father," Angelina said again. "Was at Scarvo's that night." She motioned to Greta who retold what she had seen.

"It seems your father gets around, Miss Poulos."

Angelina sighed. "He always did."

"He's proving to be a big problem for us too. We're going to have a chat with our superiors to see what can be done about it."

"Deported back to Santorini would be nice," she said.

"Maybe we can arrange that." Burns nodded. "We'll be seeing you." They left, and everyone started talking at once.

"Good heavens, what sort of father do you have?" Carson asked.

"At least you're not hurt, just a few little scratches, we can cover those," Stephanie said.

"Hope the merchandise wasn't damaged," Thomas added.

"I am so sorry," Greta said. "We will check into every owner we hire from in future. No more drug dealer houses. In fact, for the next movie we move into the city into a building with one hell of a view. Oh, we've spliced together the movie already and it is hot, hot, hot."

"Already?" Pedro asked. "I only filmed it last night."

"Oh, please." Greta waved a hand. "It was so hot we spliced it together in no time, but the final movie won't be done for a few days. You'll be able to film next week, won't you? We want to release it after the Porn Star Awards."

"I think we should release it sooner," Carson piped up. "Capitalise on the fact your brother's new movie is out and doing shamelessly well."

"Speaking *of* your brother," Greta added. "We do want to capitalise on the fact he *is* your brother and want to change your name, for the movie, of course, to Pedro Stefan. We might even say on the box *younger brother of Carlo*. How does that sound?"

Pedro exchanged an amused glance with Angelina. "You want me to change my name for the movies?"

"Yes."

He shrugged. "Okay."

"And you don't mind if we capitalise on you being Carlo's younger brother?"

"Well...I am." He grinned.

"Oh, good. We'll get that going next week, and we'll see you next Saturday night. Let's go and leave these lovebirds alone." Greta ushered the others out and left Pedro and Angelina to themselves.

The loved-up duo glanced at each other and grinned.

"Hello, Mr Stefan."

"Hello, Miss Poulos."

*****

Monday morning, Burns and Devron talked to their captain who called in Detective Gardo. He'd liaised between the drug division and the mob squad, bringing down some of the city's drug dealers and mobsters.

"What have you got for me?" The six feet of Giancarlo Gardo drove full bore into the precinct. He was as wide as a Mack Truck and as angry as a bull in a china shop.

"Nedro Scarvo," was all Captain Shield said.

Gardo stopped, eyes wide. "You got the son of a bitch?"

"Not quite," Shield said. "But you need to hear a story that might help you get him. Burns." He waved the officer over. "Tell him what you told me."

Burns told the whole story, a very detailed story, about a poor Greek boy who had been harassed by his girlfriend's father who just happened to know Scarvo. He told of finding drugs after Pedro spent the night filming a movie and how he'd had his brakes cut.

"But do you have any evidence on *him*?" Gardo asked. "It's all well and good to have people's say so, but we need cold hard facts."

Burns shook his head. "Except for the block of coke, no. But we do have Poulos charged with assault and attempted rape. He's in complete denial that he's done anything wrong, but he *will* do anything to get rid of Stephanopoulos, including cutting brakes and leaving coke in the car."

"Well, that's Scarvo's MO," Gardo said. "We've seen it before. So if they're in cahoots, we'd better put a tail on this Poulos and anyone associated with him."

"He did have a frequent visitor in the hospital," Devron added.

"Put a tail on him too." Gardo made for the door. "And one on this Stephanopoulos kid. Who knows what *he's* up to?"

*****

Andros scoured Monday's paper, but all he found was a small snippet about *Studio 69*'s resident DJ crashing his car. That he was okay and doing fine.

"What? Doing fine! Why isn't he dead, or arrested, or in jail?" Andros reread the article in case he'd missed something. There was nothing about drugs or cut brakes. "Fuck!" He slammed the paper down. *"When the fuck is he going to die?"*

*****

The woman wrote down her plan. The time had come to take the bull by the horns and deal with it herself. Especially now that Pedro was in the hospital.

"With that whore," she spat. "I am alone and not with my baby's father. I am alone and not with the man I love." The fury burned in her eyes. It burned in her throat. It burned in her gut. *I don't know who that man was, but he shot at the wrong person. Oh, if only he had killed Angelina!* If that had happened, she would be at Pedro's side right now. She picked up the photo of Angelina. The face was scratched out, and there was a red target drawn over her.

"Bitch, you are going down!"

*****

Pedro was released, along with Angelina, from the hospital. Greta arrived with a limousine to take them home, but they stopped at the car dealership where he'd gotten the Corvette to buy a Mustang convertible. It was blue; the exact same shade as his eyes.

"Well, I'll let you drive home then," Greta said. "Don't forget, this Saturday we have a new movie."

"Let me know the address and I'll be there," he said, and they drove home in the brand-car to find boxes of letters and presents from adoring fans. Pedro carried them inside, and they spent the next few hours going through them.

Pedro laughed. "Bev Marie wants me to take her home to Mykonos and fuck her till she dies." He shook his head. "God what a woman."

"Just don't get any ideas," Angelina told him, pulling out a medium sized box from the bottom. "What's this, it's heavy." She lifted the lid, pulled back the tissue paper and stared…and gasped…and threw the box at Pedro. "What sort of sick joke is that? Get rid of it."

He looked up in surprise at the box and grabbed it.

Glancing inside he saw an eleven inch vibrator sliced up with red liquid all over it. "Ugh, what the hell!" He saw photos of Angelina with her face scratched out and a bullseye on her head. There was a bloody piece of paper that he pulled out. "*If you continue fucking your whore she will die. Stop seeing her and you will live. You have one chance. You have one choice. Make the right one.* What the hell! Where's the lid?" Angelina handed it to him and he jammed it on. "Clearly this is someone's sick idea of a sick joke, and we're not going to do anything about it."

"It's not like it's something we can take to the cops. New York's newest porn star gets a sliced dildo as a present. Yeah." Angelina snorted. "They'd really take that seriously."

Pedro looked at her. "Well, I know two people who will take that very seriously."

*****

"That's some gift," Eddie said the next night when Pedro showed him the box. "Wouldn't put too much thought into it, kid, but if you're worried about this and everything else, get yourself a bodyguard." They were sitting in Eddie's office before 69 opened.

Pedro sighed and sat down across from him. "I don't want to get a bodyguard."

"But with this Poulos guy trying to kill you, maybe you should. And this crazy whack job that thinks she's pregnant with your baby, what about her?"

"I don't know." Pedro ran a hand through his hair

then rested his head in his hands. "I don't know anymore. I just want to be left alone."

"Well, you won't be, and you aren't. You work here, you're doing porn now, and someone's trying to kill you. It's time to hire bodyguards for both of you. Look…" He spun through his Rolodex. "Here's the name of the company I use when I need extra protection. Think about it." He handed the card over.

Studio 69 opened, and Pedro did his thing. The news had travelled far and wide about his accident, and all of the regulars were there. Bev, Sara, Martine. Even Bridie dropped by to say hello. Diane Von Furstenberg, Dyan Cannon and Jerry Hall cornered him for a chat and asked how he was. He was very moved that so many people were interested in how he was and was very grateful for all he had. But what he had was being threatened, and he needed it to stop. He called Angie before leaving. "Anything you want me to pick up on the way home?"

"Breakfast?"

"You got it." He stopped at the little café down the road from their apartment and was home ten minutes later. "Breakfast!"

Angelina crawled out of bed, her arm still in a sling, her hair a wild mess. She was taking the week off Juilliard, although, at the rate she was going she'd get booted out before she graduated. "Yum, I'm hungry." She grabbed a fork and dug into the scrambled eggs.

"How did you sleep?" Pedro opened the two cups of coffee.

"Badly," she mumbled around her food.

Handing over a cup, he said, "Here, get this into you. You want a painkiller?" He fussed over her, making sure she had what she needed before sitting at the island bench and eating. "I talked to Eddie about the package, and he suggested getting bodyguards. I said I'd talk to you."

She finished eating a mouthful of bacon and eggs and swallowed. "For both of us?"

Sipping his coffee, he found it hot and strong just the way he liked it. "One each. Unless you want two," he joked. "What do you think?" He watched her face for any indication of a yes or no.

After eating another mouthful and drinking some coffee, she said, "Isn't it a bit late for bodyguards?" She pointed to her arm before grabbing the strip of bacon he was about to eat. "The damage has already been done." She popped the bacon in her mouth.

"But maybe we, I, can stop even more from happening. What do you say? Do you want a bodyguard?" He silently implored her with his charismatic eyes. "I love you, I want to keep you safe. And you're right; too much damage has already been done. So let me protect you from now on."

Her lips moved up into a smile. "You know I can't resist you when you stare at me with those big blue eyes."

He batted his long black lashes. "Please!"

Her laughter floated around the room. "As long as I can have a woman."

After breakfast, Pedro made a call to the company Eddie recommended and arranged for two guards who would be at his door at six.

At six p.m. he opened the door to find a man on one side and a woman on the other, standing like sentinels outside the door. "Hello, hey, come in and we'll have a chat."

The man was Pedro's height, with a big build and cropped black hair. The woman was average height, with blonde hair pulled into a bun. They both wore suits.

"Right, I'm Pedro Stephanopoulos, and I guess you will be my bodyguard," he told the man.

"Mark Monroe, ex-special forces, black belt in karate, weapons expert." The man shook Pedro's hand.

"Great," Pedro replied. "Do you have a problem with hanging around a club all night and the apartment all day?"

"If that's the job, sir, that's what I'll do."

"Great." Pedro nodded his enthusiasm. "And this is Angelina," he said as she walked into the room to see their new guards. "You'll be guarding her," he told the woman. "So far it's just here at the apartment, but she'll be back to school next week and we'll need to let the school know to expect you. And you are?"

"Sara-Michelle Dubois. Fifth Dan black belt and weapons specialist." She nodded.

"Great," Angelina said. "I got a woman. I hope you won't be bored here all day and night. I'm taking the week off and don't go anywhere."

"Wherever you need me to be that's where I'll be."

"Great, well…" Pedro grabbed his bag. "I need to go to the club. Now we won't be home until six-thirty in the morning, and then I sleep all day. So I don't know how that's gonna work out. If you do tandem watches, one sleeps while the other works…"

Mark gave a curt nod. "That's how we do it, sir. If that's what you need."

"Okay. Well, then we'd better get going." He kissed Angelina goodbye and left with Mark. "I've never had a bodyguard before, so I have no idea how you do it, or how this is supposed to play out."

"First thing's first," Mark said as they entered the underground car park. "I inspect your car before you get in it." He circled the Mustang, checked underneath the hood and got down under it. "All clear. Second thing is, I drive." He held out his hand.

Pedro opened his mouth to say something but rethought his decision and quickly handed over the keys. "Any reason why you get to drive my new wheels?" He slid into the passenger side. "I only just got her this week."

Mark slammed the door shut, making Pedro wince. "Because if we need a quick getaway, I know how to out-manoeuvre them. I know New York like the back of my hand. I know which roads to take if I have to get you out of the club or your apartment. I know how to get you to where you're going in the shortest time, and if the people who are after you are from out of town or out of the country, then they don't have the knowledge and I've got the upper hand."

Pedro grinned. "I'm impressed."

Mark remained poker-faced. "You should be!"

*****

Andros had no one else to turn to so he called Stavros. "Where are you?"

"In my motel."

"I need to see you. Come to my apartment now."

Twenty minutes later Stavros stood in Andros's apartment. "What now?"

"What now is that I need you to stake out 69, so you can get information on Pedro and Angelina. When they go out, what sort of car they have since the old one's obviously not working. Who comes over. I want to know every little detail so I can plan my revenge."

Stavros inwardly groaned. *Not again, fuck he's bonkers.* "When do I start?"

"Now," Andros said, looking at his watch. "He'll be at 69. I know Angelina's taking the week off Juilliard, but I still have no idea where they live, so follow Pedro home and find my daughter."

"Yes, Mr Poulos."

"And Stavros…"

"Yes, Mr Poulos…"

"Don't cock-up this time."

*****

The woman held the little baby onesie in her hands. She smelt it, drawing in a breath slowly, breathing in the scent of new clothing and new baby. Her baby. Hers and Pedro's baby.

She didn't have long to go, it was only a matter of a

few months, if that, but she needed supplies, she needed a new home, and she needed Pedro. She needed the father of her baby to provide for her. *And when he sees his newborn and holds her in his arms he's going to know that this is where he belongs,* she thought. *With us.*

Caressing her stomach, she spoke to the baby. "Not long now, Bubba. Daddy's coming to see us. He's gonna be with us real soon." She picked up another picture of Angelina with her face scratched out and sneered at it. "Bitch, your days are numbered."

She placed the photo into a gift box with her note and bloodied onesie. It would be posted later, or left somewhere they would find it. So easily find it. Like maybe outside their apartment door.

*****

Stavros knew Pedro didn't knock off work until after six so he slept until five. Getting up at the crack of dawn on a crisp fall day was not what he wanted to be doing, but he did it anyway. He drove into New York and hovered on 54th street near the alley. He checked his watch. Six-twenty. He waited. Not long now.

He watched celebrities exit the club and noticed a red-haired woman lingering near the alley. He frowned. She was the same woman in the alley that night. The one who'd gotten in the way of his clean shot at Pedro.

He watched her. She was slowly making her way down the alley to hide behind the trashcans she'd emerged from that night. In fact, now that he thought about it, she was the same woman from down the road outside of Angelina's first apartment.

Now what does she want and could she cause trouble? She saw me that night, what if she remembers me? He watched her hide and saw Pedro emerge from the back door with a man. The man checked over a blue Mustang convertible before motioning to Pedro to get into the passenger side. He got behind the wheel, and they left.

The woman came out from behind the cans and ran for the alley as he slowly drove off behind Pedro. In the rear view, he saw the woman hail a taxi. They drove down 8th Avenue and turned onto Central Park West before pulling into an apartment complex.

Stavros pulled over just past it, making sure to get the number. He watched as the gate to the underground parking closed, and a guard checked that it was locked. There was a doorman and check-in screenings. He watched a taxi drive slowly past with the woman in the back, her head frantically moving around for a look at where he lived.

Interesting. What sort of threat was she?

The taxi drove off with her looking longingly out the back window, and he followed at a safe distance, all the way back to her tacky apartment where she climbed out and went inside. He made a note of the address and drove off to see Andros.

"Well," Andros demanded when Stavros walked in the door. "Where do they live?"

Stavros pulled out his notebook. "On Central Park

West, but he had a guy with him who checked the car over before they left. And he drove it. It's a Mustang, blue, but we might have another problem."

"What's that?" Andros tightened the belt on his robe. It was seven-fifteen a.m., and he was not used to being up this early.

"The woman, the one that got in the way of the shooting, she was there again. And I remembered I'd also seen her outside of Angelina's apartment the night you were there. It looks like they have a stalker."

Andros poured himself a cup of coffee. "Interesting. Their new place, where is it from here?

"Across the park."

He sipped his coffee. "Interesting. Very interesting."

*****

Saturday rolled around and Pedro got ready for the movie. He opened the door and asked Mark and Sara-Michelle in. "I need to head off to work, but not at the club."

"Sure," Mark said. "Where are we going?"

"Downtown to a building to film a movie."

"Okay then. What kind of movie, and what kind of security do they have?"

A brief frown crossed over Pedro's face. "Well, it's filming on the roof, so I guess they'll have their own or use the building's security."

"And what kind of movie?"

Pedro winced. "A porn movie."

Mark's eyebrows slowly moved up his forehead,

and Pedro wasn't sure if he was going to laugh. But strict business won out, and Mark's expression was back to normal. "Okay then," was all he said.

"And I'm coming too." Angelina walked out of the bedroom with her bag and coat.

"No, you're not. You're going to stay here," Pedro said. "It's safer."

"No, I'm not," she told him. "I missed the last one, so there's no way I'm missing watching this one being made." She turned to Sara-Michelle. "You don't have a problem with pornos do you?"

Sara-Michelle tried to hide a smile. "No, ma'am."

"Good, it's set. We all go together."

"Oh, my God, this is so embarrassing," Pedro muttered as they gathered their things and left. They arrived at the old office building half an hour later, and after security checks, walked out of the elevator to see the whole roof had been set up like a party. Cabanas, flowing curtains, DJ booth, lights, waiters. Basically the same concept as Long Island.

"Pedro, darling." Greta and Stephanie came toward him. "We're going to have so much fun." They stopped at Angelina and the two bodyguards. "And what are you doing here?" Greta asked Angelina.

"Watching," she replied. "You didn't think I wouldn't be interested in watching my boyfriend do a porno, did you? I can't wait."

Greta frowned and turned to the others. "And they are?"

"Bodyguards," Pedro said. "Eddie suggested we hire them."

"Yes, that's a good idea," she said. "With everything that's happened you need protection. Let's walk you through what will happen." She led him onto the dance floor, and the others followed.

"The girls will be here, you will be in your DJ booth, you'll come down and start flirting with the girls. When you are having sex the camera will circle around you, and there will be one above you here." She pointed, and they all saw a camera suspended above them. "You will be standing on a record. It's a stage that's painted to look like a record that we will bring in during the movie. We'll get some awesome above shots of the three of you on the spinning record."

Pedro nodded. "Sounds cool. I hope it looks good too."

"It will. Now, let's get you downstairs and dressed."

They followed her down to the top floor, and found everyone scurrying around like worker bees. Sound and engineering were all working off to the right, and to the left was the dressing area full of beautiful women getting changed into skimpy dresses and clothes. Tits and pussy were everywhere, and Mark had the decency to look away. The girls didn't care, they just wanted Pedro.

"Pedro, darling, come and see what you're fucking later."

"Come and fuck this now, Pedro." A blonde bent over and aimed her ass at him.

He grinned cockily. "Gotta go to work, babe," he told Angelina.

"Don't worry, babe, I'll be watching," she replied.

He laughed and walked over to the women where he was swamped. They quickly had his clothes off.

"Girls," Stephanie yelled. "Leave the merchandise alone. It's for later." She escorted Pedro away from the horde to a quiet spot for him to change.

Angelina and their guards stood off to the side watching it all go down. Within half an hour they were back on the roof watching the cameras roll, standing with the other crew behind white curtains so they weren't noticed on camera. There was a screen set up in front of them so they could see what was being filmed, and so far, it was all women in the setting rays.

Pedro finally walked out in his tuxedo pants and white shirt and climbed behind the booth. He danced, he sang, he flipped records into the air and caught them behind his back before flipping them onto the players. He pulled trick after trick and Greta loved him for it.

"God, he's hot," Greta said.

"He certainly is," Angelina muttered in agreement.

"Not much of a porno yet," Sara-Michelle said.

"Just you wait," Greta told her. "Wait until he takes his clothes off."

Yes, Angelina thought. *Just you wait.*

The city lit up the skyline and the stars came out to play. Pedro's shirt came out of his pants, and he came down off the stage. Women surrounded him, but one by one he waved them off until just the two remained. Blonde twins with big tits. They were standing on the spinning record stage and started undressing each other. A dress came off, his shirt came off, a top came off, his pants came off, a skirt came off, the underwear came off.

"Jesus fucking Christ," Sara-Michelle muttered, her eyes going wide.

Angelina smiled. "Yep!"

They watched Pedro fuck one twin while sucking the other and then he changed partners. Groping, licking, gyrating occurred before they went down to their knees on the spinning record.

Not long after it was done so was he, and to a resounding applause he slipped his pants on and left the stage.

"Whoo, that's my man," Angelina called as they emerged from behind the curtain. "That was fucking hot! Can we keep that record stage?" she asked Greta.

"Um, sorry, we'll need it for future use," she replied, stunned that Pedro's girlfriend wouldn't have a problem with him doing porn. "You seemed to enjoy it," Greta said to her.

"Why wouldn't I?" Angelina looked at her. "I get that every single day. I'm secure in our relationship, so if he wants to follow his brother into this..."

"Have you seen Carlo's movie?" Greta asked.

"Last month when it came out," Angelina said. "Have you *seen* his brother? Phwoar! If I wasn't with..." She trailed off at Pedro's expression.

"Me? You'd what?" he asked, a cocky grin on his face. "Do my brother?"

"Well..." Angelina blushed. "You have *seen* your brother...right?"

"Oh, God." He laughed. "Just as well he's on the

other side of the country."

"And have you heard? He's nominated for quite a few Porn Star Awards," Greta said.

Pedro raised a brow. "Really? No, I haven't heard. But then I haven't read up on the awards, so don't know much about them, or how they work."

"You'd better." Thomas walked over to them. "Because you'll be nominated next year so get ready." He eyed off Mark whom he hadn't noticed before. "And who are you?"

"Mark Monroe, bodyguard." Mark nodded. He knew fags from a mile away and wasn't interested.

"Bodyguard, huh?" Thomas preened, moving closer to the tall brute of a man. "I wouldn't mind a good bodyguard," he flirted.

"Then get one that's interested in fags," Mark muttered loud enough for only Thomas to hear as he narrowed his eyes at the male before him. "Because *I'm not interested.*"

Thomas stepped back, shocked at the words. No one else had heard or taken notice as they were too busy talking about the porn awards. He turned and left, leaving the others wondering what had gone down.

"What happened?" Pedro asked Mark.

"I told him I wasn't interested in his advances," he replied, his face stone-cold hard. "Apparently, he doesn't like to be rejected."

Pedro frowned and glanced from Mark to Sara-Michelle who remained poker-faced, to Angelina who looked puzzled.

"We should go," Angelina finally said and turned to Greta. "Thank you for letting us stay. It was fun."

"Oh, thank you for coming," Greta replied, waving them off.

They made it downstairs for Pedro to change then went down to the car park. Mark checked the car, and they piled in.

"So, what *was* that about?" Pedro asked on the way home. "Coz whatever you said it upset him."

"As I said." Mark kept his eyes on the road. "I rejected his advances. Not my problem if he couldn't deal with that."

"It just seemed like a strong reaction to someone saying, I'm not interested."

"Sometimes people overreact." Mark pulled into the underground parking for their building. "If you're not strong enough to understand and accept the fact some people just won't be interested, then you should stop asking them."

"Fair enough," Pedro said. Climbing out, he pulled the seat forward and helped Angelina out of the back. "So, what did you think of the movie?"

"I'll tell you when we get upstairs," she whispered with a giggle.

"Can't you tell me now?" They entered the lift and went up.

"Tell you later."

They got off on their floor and walked toward their door.

"Hold up." Mark put up a hand, and Sara-Michelle drew her gun "We have a situation." Mark waved them back. "I'll check it out." He slowly moved toward the door to get a closer view of the object sitting in front of it. "It's a box. A gift box."

Angelina drew a sharp breath. "Not another one."

"What do you mean another one?" Sara-Michelle asked her.

"We got a gift box in some fan mail the other day, and it contained some not very nice things," Angie told her.

"Monroe," Sara-Michelle called. "It could be ugly fan mail, be careful."

Mark crouched and checked for wires and small devices before flipping up the lid. Pulling back the tissue paper he saw photos of Angelina with her face scratched off and a target on her head. Underneath was a bloodied baby onesie with a note. "This is sick," he said.

Pedro moved to his side. "Stay back," he told Angelina and held out his arm. "What is it?" He bent down and looked inside while Mark pulled out the note.

"You're out of time. Make your choice. Our life or her death. Your baby's life hangs in the balance. Can you really say no to our baby?"

"Is that blood?" Pedro asked.

Mark sniffed it then touched a finger to it and tasted it. "Sauce with something else." He looked at Pedro. "You, my boy, have a stalker."

Pedro stood up. "Great, that's all I need."

"Let's take this inside shall we." Mark picked up the package while Pedro opened the door and then waved

Angelina and Sara-Michelle inside.

"What is it?" Angelina asked, dropping her bag and coat on the kitchen island.

"Another one of those gifts," Pedro said as Mark dropped the box next to her bag on the counter.

"A pretty bad gift," Mark said. "You still got the other one?"

Pedro went to the hall cupboard, dug it out of the box of fan mail, and laid it next to the new one. "Same person?"

Mark examined both parcels. Same kind of box, same wrapping, same kind of note. Finally, he said, "I think it's from the same person. Now, who could this woman be?"

Pedro shook his head. "I have no idea. I came to New York with Angie. We've been together since..." He remembered back.

"You've got something?" Mark saw his faraway look.

"No." Pedro came back. "It couldn't be...she was brunette..."

"A woman can dye her hair," Sara-Michelle said.

Pedro breathed in sharply. "On Santorini, at the club, there was a woman. Brunette hair. She attacked me one night after the show. I was on the beach, I'd just had a swim, and she was standing in front of me naked. I told her I wasn't interested and walked away. She shoved me onto the sand from behind, rolled me over, ripped my pants open and tried to..." He made small hand gestures. "...you know..."

"Jump on your love muscle," Angelina stated with a straight expression.

Pedro blushed and glanced away. "Yeah. That's what we're calling it today?" he asked her before continuing. "But I pushed her off and ran for it."

"You know," Angelina said. "Now that you mention it, there was a woman who followed me home and attacked me. She had dark hair, and it was in the early hours of the morning. I karate kicked her, and she fell to the ground and called me a whore."

"Would you recognise her if you saw her again?" Mark asked. "Either of you?"

Pedro shook his head. "It was night-time."

Angelina shook hers as well. "It was dark and I didn't get a good look."

"Okay. What about since being here in New York?"

"Besides my father?" Angelina said. "Nope."

"Mmm," Pedro mumbled. "There could be…"

"What?" Mark asked. "Tell us. It could be vital to stopping this woman."

Pedro sighed and looked everywhere else but Angelina.

"What aren't you telling me?" she asked. "Spit it out."

"Ugh," he groaned. "The night of the shooting, there was that woman who was in the alley. She was shot too."

"The one that ended up in the psyche ward?" Angelina asked.

"Right, well, Stew was there when she was loaded into the ambulance, and according to him, she muttered, *'my baby…Pedro's baby'…*" Pedro winced at the words.

Angelina's brows hit her hairline. "She what?"

"Don't look at me like that." He shook his head and put his hands up in protest. "I have no idea who she is or what she's up to. But when Stew told the doctor about it, she was examined, and *she wasn't pregnant,* so they put her in the psyche ward for observation in case the blow to her head knocked something loose."

"And maybe they were already loose," Mark said.

"What do you mean?" Pedro asked him.

"What if this is the same woman?" He pointed at the gifts. "This woman from Santorini becomes fixated on you, getting you to fuck her to get her pregnant." He waved a hand at Angelina. "She hates you, so attempts to do something, and now she's popping up here in New York leaving gifts about 'Angelina must die for your baby'. I reckon it's the same whack job and we need to find her."

"How do we do that?" Angelina asked.

Mark checked the boxes. "I'll dust for prints, eliminate ours, see who else's is on this stuff. Take more notice of who's hanging around now. I'm looking for a woman with red hair."

"Oh, my God." Pedro snapped his fingers. "I bet it's the same woman at the club that night. She got into a fight with Martine Krevnokov, but she got her in a headlock and security threw her out. Oh, my God, I forgot about that."

"Wow," Angelina said. "She really is in our life."

"And now it's time to get her out," Mark said.

*****

It took a couple of days for Stavros to finally resolve the issue that was going on between his orders from Andros and his guilty feelings. He wasn't sure if spying on Pedro and Angelina was even right. His conscience was getting the best of him, and he wasn't sure what to do about it.

Did he follow through with the orders, or walk away? And if he did walk away, what would Andros do to him? If he *didn't* walk away, two young people would be dead.

He paced across his hotel room. He knew where they lived. Knew where they worked. Knew how far by foot their apartment was from across the park. Knew which path to take to not be seen. Knew which path to take to get there quickest.

Yes, he had done all the legwork, the dirty work, while Andros sat back in his luxurious apartment and waited while his lawyer got him off his charges.

Stupid bastard!

Unless he bribed his way out, there was no way he'd be leaving for Santorini. Unless he paid every person up the food chain, he'd be sent to jail. But then Andros Poulos was a wealthy man. If he wanted to pay a thousand people off, he could quite easily do so with drugs, money, sex; anything they wanted he could *and would* pay them off with.

He didn't know when he was supposed to do it. Kill Pedro that is. And he didn't know *how* he'd be asked to do it, but he knew without a doubt his boss would walk away scot free with clean hands and he'd be left paying for it with his life. His hands would be the dirty ones.

He looked down at them. They were clean, reasonably anyway. They already had the shooting on them; did he want anything else to mar them and make them dirty?

"Argh!" he cried and rubbed his forehead. "I don't know if I can do this. I really don't know." His pace picked up. *I can't kill those two kids.* The first time had been bad enough and that hadn't worked, but wounding that woman and Angelina had scarred him. Never mind the fact that Andros had gone off on him for shooting his daughter.

His daughter. *Puh-leeze! That's if she's even his daughter considering what he did to her. Ugh, my stomach. Hearing what that bastard did to her from his own lips. So proud of the abuse. Not caring that she is only an eighteen-year-old girl that he raised as his own.*

He bit his lip. It had sickened him to the pit of his core, and he'd wanted to kill Andros there and then. But he had refrained. Oh, how barely had he refrained. He knew something needed to be done, but didn't know what.

The phone rang…

*****

"What have you been up to?" Pedro asked Wednesday morning after getting home. Dumping his bag on the end of the bed he saw Angelia reading a magazine. He glanced at his watch. "Six-forty and you're awake reading a magazine."

She looked up. "I don't have school today. I'm

taking a break, two days on, one off, two days on, so I'm waiting for you."

"What are you reading?" He flopped on the bed beside her and peered at the article. "Carlo Stefan, the hottest new cock in the business. Ah, Jesus!"

"I've been reading up on your brother." She flipped the magazine over to reveal the cover. "It's *Porn Star Monthly* from last month. It has stories on the nominees for the awards and your brother is up for a lot—"

"He always was," Pedro muttered.

She giggled. "As best male newcomer, his movie is up for best movie, best director, best producer, and he's up for best cock and best actor. You know he wrote some of the Cabana movies. There's four or five of them, and it says here he got a pay raise for writing them. Babe…" She closed the magazine. "Maybe you should get into writing *your* movies? You'd get a pay rise. Ask Greta about it."

Pedro stared at the magazine and his brother's blue eyes. Just like his. Just like their mother's. He swallowed, but teared up anyway. "Oh, God, I miss them," he sobbed.

Angelina wrapped her good arm around him, resting his head on her chest. "Shh, it's okay. I know you do baby, I know you do."

He sobbed until he was done and then freshened up. A shower did him good, and breakfast would be even better. Hearing Angie in the kitchen, he spied the magazine on the bed and sat down to flick through it. He read snippets about his brother on several pages until he came to the story. The picture was of him in a pool, soaked through wet. He grinned. It would get all the girls wet. If there were a wet t-shirt contest for guys, he'd definitely win hands down. He read the story.

'I miss my family like crazy. One minute we were all together on Mykonos and the next I'm in Hollywood making movies. My two little brothers have flown the coop to go and do their thing, and I haven't seen them since June. Four months isn't long, but it feels like forever.'

Pedro felt the tears again. Wasn't he in the same boat right now? He'd left in July and not gone back. Reading the rest of the article, he saw there was no mention of why he'd left. He thought about it. *I wonder why the charges were dropped. I guess I won't know unless I see him.*

*****

The woman lay in bed trying to keep cool. It was mid-October, but the heat still lingered some days, not to mention the noise outside. How could people sleep with that racket outside?

Rolling over, she stared at the corkboard with all of Pedro's pictures on it. What had become of Andros Poulos? She had seen him go into Angelina's apartment last month, but had followed Angelina so had no idea what had happened since.

Except that someone was trying to hurt her Pedro. Was it Andros? Had he ordered a hit on Pedro instead of taking his whore of a daughter home? Maybe she should track him down and have a little chat with him. He clearly wasn't doing his job as her father. He should have taken her by the ear and dragged her home by that fancy private jet of his. But no, he'd stuck around and Angelina had been bruised. Had he done that to her? Had he taught her a lesson? She hoped so.

Sitting up, she swung her legs to the floor. *Oh, Pedro, I need you. Why won't you come to me and our baby? Our baby needs you, we need you. That whore doesn't. And don't you know he's trying to kill you? How can you be with a whore whose father is trying to kill you? I wouldn't do that to you. I wouldn't hurt you. I love you.*

She went over to the board and stroked the photos one by one. "I love you, I would never hurt you. I need you to be a father to our baby." She kissed one of the photos. "I love you, you will be mine. Soon, very soon. We will be together very soon. Not long now, baby." She stroked her stomach. "Not long now until your papa is here and we will be married and be a happy little family." She felt the baby move. "Oh, yes, little one. We will be a happy little family soon. Very soon indeed. Just a matter of days and daddy will be leaving that whore he's with and coming home to us."

She left the board and slipped out of her nightshirt. It was Pedro's, and she'd taken it on one of her many visits to their first apartment. He didn't seem to miss it, and it smelled of him still. It made her feel closer to him, that he was closer to their baby.

Stepping into the shower, she thought about her plan and how she was going to execute it. Yes, the plan had to go off without a hitch. Because if anyone got in her way it would be damaging to all involved and she couldn't have anything happening to Pedro before she got to him.

Down on the street below, Stavros was gazing up at the apartment wondering what he was going to do with her.

Twenty-five feet away, Mark was wondering what he was going to do with them both.

Stavros had been given the address by his boss. Not Andros, who was just a small time boss, but his big boss. He'd been given a plan, a plan that involved a lot more than what Andros had made him do. He'd been given clear orders and had to follow them to a T. He had to get the woman out of the way and then Andros out of the way. And he'd been told by any means necessary.

He glanced up and down the street and spotted the man that had been with Pedro looking up at the same apartment. "Fuck! What's he doing here?" He took off in the opposite direction and made it down the street to his car. Seeing Mark in the rear view, he took off.

"Not so fast, buddy boy." Mark was parked right behind him and drove off, not wanting to lose him. Following at a safe distance, he tailed him to Jersey to a small hotel, and pulling up to the curb, watched the man go inside. "Well, now. What are you up to?"

*****

Pedro stared at the ceiling. It was eight-forty, and normally he'd be asleep. But today he couldn't. Something was wrong. He felt it in his bones. He wasn't sure if it was Carlos's article, or the fact he had left in such a rushed way. But it wasn't *just* the fact they had all left. It was something bad. Something bad was going to happen. He didn't know what, he didn't know when. He just knew soon.

He heard Angelina in the lounge room. She was studying on the couch, keeping as quiet as she could, but he still heard her. Still heard the page of her book being turned. Still heard every intake of breath, every sigh.

"Jesus!" He rolled out of bed and sat up. Ah, the life of a DJ. Work all night, can't sleep all day. And he certainly wasn't interested in taking pills. He'd learned a bad enough lesson on Santorini when he'd found his juice was being spiked by Andros. No, he wouldn't be taking sleeping pills.

But it kept nagging. *Maybe I should go home and see my parents? Is that it? But then Andros would just follow me there.*

No, he had to sort this out, whatever it was, and he had a feeling it was coming soon.

*****

Greta sat looking at the photos of Pedro. "My, God, he's gorgeous." The shots from Long Island had turned out beautifully, and she put a few aside to be used for promotional posters and video covers. "Speaking of..."

She grabbed the video of the movie and popped it into the VCR. She sped through until they got to the sex. "Oh, God, you do it so well," she murmured.

Pedro's eleven inches was one inch bigger than his brother, and she wondered if they'd ever measured off against one another. She'd seen Carlo's movie, and while it was hot, Pedro's was hotter, classier, and tasteful.

She'd heard him briefly mention a middle brother and wondered if he was like them. "Oh, yes, this movie will be the talk of the town at the porn awards next year." They had just been, and Carlos had won almost all of them. "Oh, yes, Harry, I'm going to beat you next year. I'm going to beat you with Pedro Stefan. He's got two inches in height and one inch in cock on your boy." An idea came to her. *Well, maybe that idea will work once Pedro finishes his movies. I'll have a little chat with him.*

*****

Mark kept an eye out for the two stalkers Wednesday night while Pedro was at work. It all went off without a hitch. Bev, Sara and Martine were front and centre as always, other fans stopped by, but no one tried anything. Standing just offstage near Pedro, he certainly copped an eyeful.

Men on men, women on women, sex, drugs, snorting, drinking. "Fucking hell," he muttered when two men with nothing but leather cock covers on walked by. He rolled his eyes. *The fucking jobs I have to do.* His eyes moved around the room looking for stage jumpers. The security at the door kept unmentionables out, and the extra security standing guard at the back door kept trespassers away.

So far, so good.

*****

The woman wrapped one last parcel. This time it was a dead doll with the eyes poked out and the face scratched off. It had long black hair and was covered in blood. With it was a note.

She took a cab down to their apartment and watched from down the road. "Please stay here and wait," she told the driver.

Seeing no guard at the door, she slipped in quietly and walked up seven flights of stairs. Peering around the corner, she saw no one on guard at their door. She slipped her shoes off, tiptoed along in stockinged feet, and laid the box at the door.

Smiling, she quickly ran back to the stairs, grabbed her shoes, and ran down to the lobby where she put them on, flew past the guard, who was back, and out to the taxi. "Drive," she ordered.

*****

Stavros turned down the alley beside 69. If he was going to fulfill the plan his boss had given him, then he needed to get his shit together.

"Fuck!" He saw the security guards and drove by. If they stopped him, he'd say he was taking a short cut.

But they didn't, so he looked for a place to park away from the door.

If he was going to do it, he had to do it right. No cock-ups this time. He had to be close enough to the door of Pedro's car so he could get the job done without being seen, blocked in, or stuck. He needed a quick clean getaway and needed it all to go smoothly.

Turning down 8th Avenue, he decided to leave it until the following morning, knowing he'd have a better chance of scoping it out in daylight and without the guards.

*****

Andros knew he had to put his plan into action within the next two days. He was due in court next Monday. He had no idea why; something to do with assaulting his daughter, but he knew the plan needed to happen now.

He sat staring out into the beautiful October night. It was lovely this time of the year. The air was crisp in his nostrils, the wine crisp in his mouth. Yes, it was very nice here indeed. *I'll have to consider holidaying here during fall more often. A nice summer home in the Hamptons, a fall home in the city. Yes, very nice indeed.*

Gazing across the park toward their apartment, he wondered what Angelina was doing. Had she thought about him? He knew she'd had the day off school, he knew she had a bodyguard as did Pedro. Now, it was just a matter of getting them in a place together where his plan could come to fruition. "Let's hope Stavros does his part," he muttered.

****

Pedro had to deal with a drunken Bev Marie.

"I luv you sho mush," she slurred. "I don't get drunk over just anyone ya know."

He laughed and removed her arms from around his neck. "That's nice to know Bev, but look at all the gorgeous men here in their short shorts and rock-hard abs. You can have your pick."

"I did have my pick." She weaved against him on the dance floor during a break when he'd gotten down with the crowd to dance. "I picked you."

"Why?" he asked. "Why me?"

"Because you're young, gorgeous and have a huge cock."

"And how do you know that?"

"Look at you." She eyed him up and down. "You pack a lot into those shorts, and now with your movie being released, I can't wait to see it in action. But really..." She slobbered on him. "I want to see it in action now." She grabbed his shorts, but he grabbed her hands and waved the security guards over.

"Time to go, Bev, you've had a long one."

"Will you come with me?" She was escorted away. "*Come* with me, Pedro, make me come."

"Bye, Bev." He waved and smiled at Sara and Martine, a few others gathered around, and he danced through the twelve inch with them until it was time to get back on stage. He ended the night a few hours later with another twelve inch and walked off. "Oh, God," he cried as he walked into the staff room. "Those women are ca.ray.zy!" He pulled on his t-shirt.

"You don't know the half of it," Mike said, tying a shoe lace. "They will snort anything, drink anything, suck anything."

"Such as?" Pedro asked with a raised brow.

"My cock," Mike said.

"You're kidding?"

Mike laughed. "I've had quite a few offers, but have been a gentleman and refused them all."

"Well, that sounds *so unlike* you." Pedro pulled on his jeans. "You went hell for leather when we first opened."

"I did, but then I met someone special." Mike slammed his locker shut and grabbed his bag. "And she's pretty damn special."

"Ah, sweet on someone. Who's the lucky girl, and how long's it been happening?" Pedro slid into his sneakers.

"Maggie."

Pedro looked up in surprise. "Angelina's Maggie?"

"Yep." Mike's grin was ear to ear.

"Since when?"

"Since your brother's movie. We got talking and…" He shrugged. "It happened."

"Well, good for you." Pedro high-fived him. "When are you seeing her again? Maybe we can double date."

"Not sure. I got next week off, but she's got a test at school, so maybe this weekend."

"I'll tell Angie and see if she can set something up."

"Okay. See you tomorrow." Mike walked out.

Pedro picked up his bag and met Mark in the hallway. "Time to go home. I'm beat." They left, and Mark did the usual check of the car before driving home. The parcel met them at the door.

"Ah geez, not another one." Pedro stopped as Mark investigated.

He picked it up and removed the lid. The bloodied doll and note lay inside. *"Your time is up. If you have not chosen us and our baby by Friday night, the whore's life will end."*

"What the hell?" Pedro took a step back. "I am so sick and tired of this, Mark. When will it stop?"

"Friday."

"What?"

"She says it will end Friday. So we have two days."

"Do you know who she is?"

"Yes."

"Then why haven't you stopped her?"

"With what? I'm a bodyguard, and she hasn't physically threatened you or come near you."

"She was here…tonight…with Angie here."

"Yes, but no harm was done."

"We don't know that."

Sara-Michelle opened the door. "What's going on? I can hear you inside." She saw the box. "Fuck! When did that come?"

"Is Angie okay?" Pedro asked.

"She's fine." Shaking her head, she went on. "I heard nothing all night. I have no idea when that was delivered."

"The problem is, it *was* delivered. That means she can still get into the building even with the guards and security. And that's not a good thing," Mark said.

"So, what do we do?" Pedro stared at the box.

"We keep the two of you together in the same place at the same time. Two of us protecting you is better than one. If she wants you, she'll get all of us. Four against one are not odds in her favour."

"And what about *our* odds?" Pedro asked.

"I'll make sure those odds get better. Far better than hers," Mark replied.

Pedro sighed. "This needs to end."

"It will."

*****

By Friday, Pedro was so on edge he was snapping at Angelina.

"What the fuck is going on?" She pulled him up on his behaviour after school.

"I'm sorry." He took hold of her arms. "I'm sorry. I'm just…"

"Scared about what's going to happen," she finished the sentence.

He looked into her eyes. "What do you know?" he asked slowly.

"That that psycho bitch left another present and it's all going to end tonight. Yeah…" She nodded. "I heard you all in the hallway yesterday."

"Jesus, Angie." Pedro swiped a hand through his hair. "We were trying to keep that from you."

"Why?" she demanded. "The bitch wants me dead, I have a right to face her and defend myself. Besides, *we* have bodyguards."

"But *we* don't know when she's going to strike or what she'll do," Pedro reminded her.

Angelina moved her left arm. "Can't be any worse than what my father did."

Pedro sighed. "Aw, babe, come here." He enveloped her in his arms. "I'm sorry you have to go through all of this because of me."

She pushed away and whacked him on the arm. "It's not because of you, you idiot. It's because of my father. So how bad can *she* be?"

"I just hope we don't find out."

*****

The woman had packed up her things. She didn't have much, so it all fitted into her suitcase and large overnight bag. Between her clothes and the baby's things, she was leaving with more than she'd come with, and it was all happening tonight.

She would be moving into Pedro's tonight. That whore would finally be out of the way, and Pedro would be all hers. Hers and the baby's.

She left the apartment forever, taking a taxi to Pedro's place, arriving just as they left. She told the cab driver to continue onto 69 knowing that it would soon be happening. She'd be in Pedro's arms and soon be Mrs Stephanopoulos. She was so lost in her dreams she didn't see the car following.

*****

Stavros had prepared his kit, packed his bags, and checked out of the hotel. He wouldn't be hanging around anymore, he had his orders to do the deed and get the hell out of there, and he had two days to get to his destination.

He drove into New York and waited down the road from Pedro's, watching as they drove off, surprised to see four people in the car, but not surprised to see a red-haired woman in a taxi drive past and follow the Mustang.

He followed the taxi.

*****

Andros dressed. It wouldn't be happening for hours, but he wanted to be ready. A slick light grey suit with black shirt and silver tie was going to get him into 69. He was going to see for himself Pedro's debauched lifestyle and was going to stick around until the deed was done.

*****

Mark parked opposite the back door, and he and Sara-Michelle ushered Pedro and Angelina in quickly. The sun was setting, casting shadows amongst the buildings, and Mark came back out to scour the alley. He checked behind trash cans, over fences, and around other cars. When he was satisfied, he went back inside.

178

*****

The woman paid the taxi driver and climbed out. It was a quarter to seven, and she would be waiting outside for him when he finished work. Maybe even sooner.

She spied the Mustang, but kept walking down the alley. It was ridiculous to think a pregnant woman should be carrying her own case and bag, but she had to get it done.

Moving past the car, she found a safe spot behind an old brown clunker, put her luggage down, and sat on her case to wait. She pulled a sandwich out of her handbag. It was going to be a long night.

*****

Stavros crawled to a stop in the street and saw the alley was free and clear of guards. Shifting gears, he cruised past the back door and found a nice tree to park under. He had a long wait ahead and decided to go for some food. Checking the alley, he got out, locked the car, and then walked in the opposite direction.

*****

The woman saw the car cruise by and park under a tree. Saw the man get out and walk away, and knew that was the man that had shot at them. She thought about calling the police to have him arrested, but that would put her in it. She thought about slashing his tyres, but then what if they needed a getaway car? Munching on her sandwich, she thought about it some more.

*****

Andros rolled up to the club at ten p.m., went inside, had a look around, sipped a drink, and left. Sitting in his limousine, he waited for the festivities to roll around.

*****

Stavros looked at his watch. Ten p.m. He left the café and slowly walked back to his car. He spied the two guards at the door and wondered how to proceed. Carefully crossing the alley, he walked, hunched over, to not be seen, completely missing the woman who had seen him coming and hidden between two cars.

He slid down to the Mustang, got on the ground, got underneath and cut the brake line. Being just as careful when he left, he slid down the alley toward his car only to be caught by her.

"What are you doing to Pedro's car?" she whispered furiously.

Startled, he covered her mouth with his hand and took her to the ground. "You be quiet or I'll shoot you again." He opened his jacket to reveal a gun. "Scream, and you die."

Her eyes widened and she nodded.

He removed his hand. "Now, what are you doing stalking Pedro Stephanopoulos?"

"I'm not stalking him," she whispered. "We're going

to be together. I'm having his baby, and we're going to be together tonight."

"You do know Angelina's here?"

That took her by surprise. "No, no I didn't."

"And their guards."

A steely look of determination came over her face. "*I will be* with Pedro tonight."

"Then you'll also have Angelina's father to deal with."

Now she was stunned. "Mr Poulos is here? At the club?"

"Yep."

"Is he here to take that whore home?"

"Possibly, but then I'd say he's here to kill Pedro." An idea was forming in his mind. Andros Poulos needed stopping, and he had been given the task. But maybe he could keep his hands clean and get this girl to do the dirty work.

"What do you mean, here to kill Pedro?" she spat. "He was supposed to come and take his whore home, *not kill my man.*"

"Well, that's what he's planning. You see that limo across the road from the alley?" He nodded toward it, and she turned to stare. "That's his car. He's just waiting for Pedro to get into his car and kapooh." He made an explosive sound and moved his hands apart to demonstrate a bomb blowing up.

"He's going to blow Pedro up?" Her eyes flooded with tears.

"It will go off shortly after. It has to warm up," he lied. "I was hoping to stop him, but he has my family locked away and is threatening to kill them if I don't co-operate."

"He wants you to kill Pedro?"

"Yes."

"No. I won't let that happen. Tell me what I can do."

*****

The night went off like clockwork. Sara-Michelle kept Angelina in Stew's office, and Mark kept a watch over Pedro. Come six-thirty in the morning everyone was ready to go home, including Stavros and the woman.

Stavros sat up in his seat. Any minute now. He woke the woman sitting beside him. He'd allowed her to sleep in his car, her luggage on the back seat. She stirred. "It's showtime. Now we get our revenge."

She sleepily nodded, wiped her eyes, and stepped out into the cold dark alley. The sun was not yet up, even though the light was changing shades, so the alley was cast in haunting shadows. She slipped down the alley as Stavros quietly got out and deposited her luggage next to the tree. He popped the trunk, but kept it down and then got back in the car, ready for the moment.

Mark came out first and checked the Mustang over. He got in, gunned the engine and pulled out into the alley, but alighted, leaving the door wide open and the engine running, while he went to open the club's back door for the others.

Across the street from the alley, Andros rolled down his window to see what was happening. With butterflies in his stomach, he exited the car, closed the door and stood to watch. He wanted to see their faces when they saw him because it would be the last time for any of them.

*****

At the police station, Burns and Devron got a call about a limousine sitting outside of 69 all night. They thought nothing of it until tracking it down and seeing it was rented by Andros Poulos. They called Gardo and got him out of bed. "He's at 69, his daughter's got a restraining order on him, and he shouldn't be near Stephanopoulos," Burns said.

"Right, get down there. I'm on my way."

*****

The Mustang sat idling in the alley as Pedro, Angelina, and Sara-Michelle stepped out of the club.

Something inside the woman snapped, and it snapped again when she spied Andros standing at his limousine. "No one's going to kill my Pedro," she mumbled and started screaming. "He's here, look, it's Andros Poulos, he's here!"

Pedro, Mark, Angelina and Sara-Michelle looked from the screaming woman who was running up to them on their left, barely recognising her as the stalker, to Andros Poulos on their right staring at them with a smug then confused expression on his face.

"Get back inside," Mark yelled, the Mustang forgotten.

But it was not forgotten by the woman. She jumped into the driver's seat, revved the engine and gunned it down the alley. She passed a stunned Mark.

He stopped in surprise and looked back to see everyone still standing there, then whipped his head around to watch and took off running.

The woman raced full speed for Andros, who stood shocked to the spot, and rammed right into him, smashing into the side of the limousine.

The top of his body flew backwards, arms outstretched like Jesus on the cross, his head hitting the roof of the limo, his bottom half pinned between both cars. Gravity got the better of him and he slumped onto the hood of the Mustang.

Dead.

The woman had smashed her head against the steering wheel and driver's window. Her neck was broken. Her eyes stared wide and lonely at the floor beside her.

No one in America would miss Barbara Weston; the young Australian girl who went to school with Carlos back home and was royally rejected by him. The young girl who had reconnected with him in Mykonos, even though he hadn't recognised her. The young girl who was put in her place by model Vivian Villiers and dumped by Carlos after a good fucking. She'd gone crazy after that; after he'd left the island. She latched onto Pedro, hoping he would be the father of her baby. The baby she was never actually having.

No, no one in America would miss Barbara Weston.

Mark skidded to a halt in shock at what lay before him.

Stavros had turned the car on and stepped out, leaving it running, leaving his door open, pulling the trunk up as he passed. The sound of the crash had muffled it all.

"Daddy," Angelina yelled, pulling out of Pedro's arms and bolting for the car.

Sara-Michelle ran after her as Pedro stood in shock. Staff members came from the back door, saw the carnage, and ran to help, leaving Pedro alone.

This suited Stavros perfectly, and he shoved his gun into Pedro's back. "Don't say anything. Just do as you're told, and you won't get hurt."

Pedro glanced dazedly at him as he was pulled around by the arm and led down the alley.

Burns and Devron pulled up behind Gardo on West 54th.

"Well…" Gardo strode over to the wreckage. "Looks like we don't have to worry about Poulos anymore." He eyed the body and watched Angelina on the other side of the car. "After what he did to you you're *still* crying over him?"

She stared up through tear-filled eyes, unable to say anything.

Mark pulled out of the Mustang's driver's window and turned around to come face to face with Gardo and the officers. "You'll find this woman to be a stalker. She was stalking Pedro and sending *little gifts* if you know what I mean."

"Wonderful," yelled Gardo. "Two birds with one 'stang."

"Except I think there's a third." Mark looked down

the alley. "Pedro?" He noticed a man turn around as he was smacking Pedro over the head and dumping him in his trunk. "Pedro," he yelled. "Quick, someone's got him." He raced down the alley with the officers on his tail, missing the car by inches as it sped down the alley. "Fuck," Mark spat, getting the license plate and memorising it.

Gardo screeched to a halt beside him. "*You* get in," he told Mark. "You two..." he directed the officers, "get your car and follow."

Mark jumped in, and they took off.

Burns and Devron radioed for backup at the crash site, made it to their car, and raced down the alley. Gardo came through on the radio five minutes later.

"We're after a black Cadillac Seville, license PMS 333, on Broadway...wait...it just turned onto the George Washington Bridge into Jersey." He shoved the radio back. "Now, tell me...who are you and what the fuck is going on?"

Mark gave him a sideway stare. "Mark Monroe, ex-special forces, black belt in karate, weapons expert. Hired as a bodyguard by Pedro Stephanopoulos after everything that Andros Poulos had done to him."

"No surprise there." Gardo gunned it down the highway. He saw a cop car roar up behind with sirens and lights going and radioed through. "Whoever is behind me cut the lights and sirens."

They turned off and then a voice crackled over the radio. "It's Burns and Devron, sir."

"Go on," he told Mark.

"It also turns out Mr Stephanopoulos was being

stalked by one Barbara Weston, the woman in the car. So between her and Poulos, there was a lot of damage going on."

"And the guy we're following?"

"Small time crook who gets hired by whoever needs him. Andros had him shoot at Pedro, but the woman and Angelina got in the way. Now I think there's someone bigger involved. Clearly, someone who wants Pedro Stephanopoulos."

"Any idea why?"

"Not a one."

"Any idea where he's headed?"

"Not a one."

*****

Back at the club, Eddie thanked God they'd been closed as the clean-up was going to be horrendous and take too much time. There was dealing with cops, giving statements, and waiting for the tow truck to come and clear the mess away. But that wouldn't be until later in the day, and he hoped they'd still be able to open, albeit with their stand-in DJ. Fuck knows what the hell was going on with Pedro, and why someone would want to take him! *Fuck.* He ran his hand through his receding hair. *Just another thing to deal with.*

After Angelina had given her statement to the officers, she was taken home by Sara-Michelle. She walked in, sat on the sofa, and stayed there, sitting in shock. Sara-Michelle made tea, but it sat cold in front of her as she hadn't touched it. Didn't want it. Just wanted Mark to find Pedro and bring him home. She just wanted Pedro and nothing else.

Sara-Michelle stepped aside and called her boss, fearful for her co-worker whom she had a slight crush on. "Any word on Mark?"

*****

Gardo sped down the highway, but kept a safe distance from the car. It was now daylight, and he was going to need to stop for gas.

Burns and Devron had stopped earlier and were ten minutes behind. He radioed every other cop car and police unit to be on the lookout and to stay close behind, but not scare him.

"He's just pulled into a gas station on Highway 80 in Pennsylvania," a cop called in.

Gardo slowed down. They were on the same highway and would catch up quick. Within minutes they had the station in sight and slowed down further. The car drove out and back onto the highway. Gardo drove in for gas and radioed in. "He's just left the station. We need to fill up, keep an eye on him." Five minutes later they were back on the road doing double time to catch up.

"Any idea where he's going?" Gardo asked Mark.

"Not yet."

*****

Stavros put the pedal to the metal. He needed to get the

kid out of his car as soon as possible. The longer he was in there, and the longer he was in America, the more trouble he'd be in.

He bit into a sandwich he'd grabbed at the station. He was starving, but couldn't stop to eat. Needing to be at his final destination that night, he made it into Ohio around lunchtime.

*****

Angelina still sat on the couch. It was past lunchtime, and she just sat and stared. Even when the officers who'd taken her statement came to see her for a follow-up. Even when her lawyer had come to see her about the charges against her father. She'd just sat and stared. There was so much going through her mind.

Why had her father done this? Why had the woman done what she'd done? Wasn't *she* the stalker? Why had she changed her mind and killed her father instead? Why? Why? Why was this happening?

She relived the scene. Walking out of the club, a woman screaming on their left and seeing her pointing to their right. Seeing her father with his smarmy Cheshire cat grin standing next to his limousine, as though he had no worries in the world. As if nothing mattered. Hearing the Mustang gun it down the alley. Seeing it smash into her father. Seeing his dead body.

She finally moved.

Moved into the bathroom to throw up.

*****

Stavros made it into Indiana mid-afternoon and stopped for more gas. He looked around. He knew someone would be after him, but so far saw no cars that had been behind him the whole time. He checked his watch. He'd need to step on it to make it on time. Consulting a map, he found a shortcut to take.

*****

Gardo and Mark were only five minutes behind and catching up, until needing to stop for gas. "I just saw a black Cadillac Seville, licence PMS 333, turning off the main highway onto some backroad," came through on the radio.

Gardo got out to pump gas. "It's gonna be hard to follow him now."

Mark alighted and spread the map on the roof of the car, following the back road to its destination. "Chicago."

"What?" Gardo hung up the pump.

"The road leads to Chicago." Mark folded the map. "Let's go."

*****

Pedro came to in the trunk. His head was splitting with pain and he groaned. "What the hell?" Breathing in, he choked on oily rags and dirty clothes. He felt about and found he was lying on something rectangular. His fingers traced one side and found a handle. It was a suitcase.

The car sped up and crossed some sort of grid, making the pain in his head worse. *"Where the hell are we? What the hell's going on?"* He vaguely remembered a gun in his back and a man telling him they needed to go. He didn't say where, but the shocking aftermath of the accident had made him unable to get his wits about him. But now he could, and he started looking for a way out.

Knowing the type of car he was in, he knew there was a lever on the inside so you could open the trunk. He felt for it with deft fingers and found it. Holding onto the trunk lid, he carefully popped the release and lifted it several centimetres to see they were on a back road in the country. The car slowed, and he held the trunk down.

"Damn it," he heard the man say. "I've got to get to hair. I've got to get to hair. Time's running out."

Alarms sounded, and the roar of a train thundered past. Pedro took his chance. Lifting the lid, he looked out. It was late afternoon, and the train continued past. He held the trunk while he slipped a leg out, allowing his body to slide with it, rolling out onto the road. His feet hit it first, and he paused before pulling the trunk down until it locked into place.

The train kept going and the noise killed his head, but it was coming to an end, and he needed to get out of the way. He looked around and scrambled for the bushes on the opposite side of the road so he wouldn't be seen out the window or in the mirror. He made it with seconds to spare as Stavros took off.

He lay panting. "Oh, God, my head." He rolled into a

sitting position and saw a car coming down the road. "Hey." Waving, he climbed unsteadily to his feet. "Hey." He fell onto the road and Gardo came to a skidding halt.

"Pedro," Mark yelled, getting out and running to him, hauling him to his feet. "Are you okay?"

Gardo flung open the rear door, and Mark helped Pedro in, then climbed in after him. "What the hell happened to you, kid?" Gardo stepped on the gas, and the door flew shut as he left.

"Shoved in a trunk at gunpoint." Pedro told his story, and Mark gave him a bottle of water. "Oh, God, my head," he sighed. "Angie…where's Angie?"

"She's okay," Mark calmed him. "Sara-Michelle's with her."

Pedro relaxed. "That's good. How is she about her father being dead?"

"Relieved I should think," Gardo said, flooring it. "Any idea where he was taking you?"

Pedro gave a slight shake of his head, but even that was too much, and the sharpness of the pain rattled around. "When we stopped for the train I heard, 'must get to hair, must get to hair'. I have no idea what that means."

Mark looked at Gardo's reflection in the rear view. "O'Hare!"

*****

It was pouring with rain as Stavros drove through Illinois and into Chicago. He had time to get to the airport, but wanted it all over and done with now. After driving through the city, he made it to O'Hare, passed through the gates and into one of the private hangars. The plane was waiting. He pulled to a stop and got out.

A man stepped out of the plane. "You are early."

"I wanted to get here early so this was all over and done with."

"Where is he?" The young man of Greek heritage descended the stairs, buttoned up his suit jacket, and smoothed his hair.

"In the trunk." Stavros removed the key from the ignition and hurried around to unlock the trunk. He stepped back beside the car. "Ready and waiting."

The man walked over and lifted the trunk, looked in and lowered it. "Where is he?"

Stavros's face fell. "What do you mean where is he? He's in the trunk." He moved back to the trunk, lifted the lid, and looked inside, seeing nothing but his luggage and dirty rags. "But he…but I…he was in there."

"But where is he *now*?" The man levelled his gun at him.

"I…" Stavros shook his head in disbelief. "No, please, I had him, I had him." The bullet seared through his body under his ribcage. "No," he rasped. "I had him…" He slumped into the trunk.

*****

Since Mark and Gardo knew where Stavros was going, they hit the sirens and lights. Burns and Devron were right behind them, roaring into Chicago's O'Hare Airport. It poured with rain, thunder clapped overhead, and lightning lit up the sky. They sped through the airport and headed for the private terminals, knowing there was no way he was taking a public flight, and belted past one after the other until they came upon the car with the driver dead and hanging out of the trunk.

"Shot through the stomach." Mark rolled him back. Thunder exploded overhead. "He must have been here for a private jet."

"Look." Pedro pointed to a man running past the hangar at the other end. He fell, and they were off and running for the door to see a small jet taking off. Sirens blasted past them, and three cars skidded to a halt.

"Looks like we're not the only ones after someone," Gardo said. He lifted his collar. "Come on boys; let's see what we've got."

The five of them ran for the group of people, but made it only half way as another group was heading in the same direction from another part of the airport off to their left.

"What the hell!" Gardo skidded to a stop with Burns and Devron behind him, guns drawn. Mark and Pedro stopped a few paces ahead. The two groups stared at each other, and a man in the other group pushed his hoodie off his head.

"Oh, my God," Pedro murmured as the man ran at him. "Tomas!" His brother flew at him and grabbed him in a bear hug.

"Pedro."

"Tomas. Oh, my God," Pedro cried, hugging him back. "Tomas!"

They didn't let go, staring as if they hadn't seen one

another in years. The cops all gathered around eyeing each other off, and the boys finally noticed they were being watched.

"Ah, this is my brother," they said at the same time.

"So, who's that then?" Gardo pointed to the first group of cops that had come tearing into the airport.

The boys turned to look in the pouring rain, arms still around each other, wiping the water from their eyes for a clearer look, to see a trench-coated man nod and point in their direction. The man beside him turned.

"Oh, my God," Pedro murmured, not believing it. He knew the man the way he knew his own brother.

About the Author

L.J. has been writing since 2006, when her first of many novels, ***The Road To Vegas,*** was born. In 2016 she created the ***Porn Star Brothers*** series about three sizzlingly hot Australian born Greek Island raised brothers who became the hottest porn stars in '70s America.

L.J. lives in Australia, loves '80s music, disaster movies, and collecting Jackie Collins books as Jackie is her inspiration and mentor.

L.J. Diva is the adult pen name for author Tiara King. You can find more about Tiara on her website; follow her on social media, or visit her publishing house, Royal Star Publishing.

Socials

tiaraking.com.au/ljdiva

royalstarpublishing.com.au

Sign up for *Tiara's* Newsletter…

Make sure you're always in the know and never miss free exclusives, the latest news, book updates, and so much more with newsletters from…

tiaraking.com.au

Have you read these?

The Porn Star Brothers Series

Carlos: Book 1
Pedro: Book 2
Tomas: Book 3
Retribution: Book 4
Porn Star Brothers
Forever
Love Never Dies
Stefan: The New Generation
DeLuca
Spiros & Jenny
And Always

The Illicit Things Series

Her
Him
Madam X

A Novel Investigation Series

Designs in Crime
A Killer Plot
Murder on the Set
A Novel Investigation (omnibus)

Or these?

NOVELS

Burning Desires
Anything for You
Falling for London
The Road to Vegas
Hollywood Dreams
The Billionaire's Dirty Little Secret

SHORT STORIES

The Body
The Perfect Plot
The Star of Your Own Crime Scene